ISBN: 978-1-9990735-6-5

Author photo by Tony Hicks

www.sandyday.ca

Birds Don't Cry

Sandy Day

Chapter 1

The late afternoon sky cast a gloom—Sylvia's favorite light for taking photographs. The storm that blasted through earlier in the day had left tree bark sodden and dark and a thick mist hung between Sylvia and the distant spring sun. Water dripped soundlessly from leaves and posts and rails, everything muffled by the heavy air. Everywhere she looked, spring colors revealed themselves in a gorky array of mosses and rusts. After dinner, Sylvia resolved, she would take her camera out to the old farms. This was her favorite time of year—the sun didn't set for hours after the evening meal.

Sylvia stopped her car to open the mailbox at the end of the driveway. She pulled out a few envelopes, the local newspaper, and a couple of Red's mail-order catalogs. Then she parked her car alongside his truck under the beech tree. Red himself was sitting in the living room, looking at a muted news channel, playing, as usual, some Creedence Clearwater Revival. Sylvia dropped the mail onto the coffee table and continued into the kitchen to start Red's dinner of fish sticks.

Minutes later, Red appeared in the kitchen doorway with a letter in his hand. "The Will's gonna be read next week."

Red's grandmother had died recently, and he and his sisters, Kaffy and Maxine, were about to inherit the old woman's property. It comprised a Victorian brick house, which had been run as an inn for decades and acres of untouched coniferous forest adjacent to the inn. Maxine, the eldest, wanted to sell it all and split the money three ways, and Red seemed to favor that idea though he was nervous in a way Sylvia had never witnessed before. He'd bitten his fingernails down to the quick until his fingers looked practically deformed. And he'd told Sylvia a thousand times that he didn't see how they could afford all the estate taxes and property taxes and untold fees that would surely mount up if they tried to hang onto the property. Red's fears, Sylvia suspected, were generated by Maxine because Red, bless his soul, didn't know the first thing about real estate or finances—he didn't give that sort of thing a second thought. She shook frozen french-fries next to the fish sticks on the baking sheet and slid it into the oven.

"We're gonna be rich!" Red sidled up behind Sylvia and rubbed against her butt. He was attempting to act like his old coltish self but she'd have none of it. Lately, he was always trying to wangle or sweet-talk her into his way of thinking. "Get away!" she swatted at Red with an oven mitt.

"Come on," he laughed. "Don't ya wanna be rich?"

Sylvia didn't answer. She was tired of the inheritance subject and she'd be glad when the will was read and the matter decided one way or the other. She disagreed with Red about what should happen to the property, and Red didn't cope well when Sylvia disagreed with him. He wanted everything to run smooth and unruffled. But life was messy sometimes.

Sylvia thought Red and his siblings ought to hold on to their family property. After all, Red's grandparents had operated an inn out of the house since the middle of the last century and Kaffy, his younger sister, was doing an admirable job running Sullivan House now. In fact, Sylvia worked with Kaffy, and she knew her sister-in-law didn't suspect her siblings were planning to sell the inn, displacing her, and forcing her to give up her plans for it. Kaffy, with Sylvia's help, kept coming up with ideas for expanding the business and keeping it going. Sylvia loved the work. It gave her just the right combination of meeting some interesting people, earning a bit of money, getting out of the house every day, and most importantly still having time to take photographs. If Red and Maxine succeeded and got their way, Kaffy would be out on her ear and that would be the end of Sullivan House. Sylvia would have to find another job, or spend all day with Red, and the way he'd been acting lately, all nervous and overbearing, she didn't relish that idea.

Before working for Kaffy, Sylvia had never held down a position for more than a month or two, usually waitressing jobs for less than minimum wage and terrible tips. And she'd tried selling kitchenware, and even lingerie, at home parties but she wasn't any good at it because she didn't have enough friends. Sylvia dreaded having to find another way to make money.

To her, Red and Maxine's plan made no sense, and Sylvia couldn't understand why Red was being so stubborn about it. In the past six months, he'd also pushed for selling the little house they lived in, after they just finished fixing it up! He claimed he wanted to move somewhere else, get a change of scenery. What was the point of that? Sylvia loved living next to the forest. She loved the surrounding countryside of falling-down farms. This was the only place she'd ever truly felt at home and she thought Red felt the same way. He'd said as much when they got married—he was content to live in the house he'd been raised in.

"What did Kaffy say when she got the letter?" Red wanted to know. Even though he seemed fixated on his plan to sell, he couldn't conceal a concern about Kaffy and what she might be thinking. "Nothing," Sylvia answered. "She didn't mention it." Red, as usual, wouldn't just talk to Kaffy himself. Sylvia had discovered that was the way in the Sullivan family. Everything was buried under the floorboards.

Sylvia cleared away newspapers and clutter from the table while Red continued to pepper her with questions, which were beginning to sound a hair paranoid. "You didn't tell her that Maxine and I are going to force the sale, did you?"

Why was this a secret? What did it matter if Kaffy knew her siblings' plans? "I didn't know it had been decided," Sylvia answered.

"Well...maybe it has." Red shifted his head, rolled it around a few times on his ruddy neck, as though to release tension. His rheumatism was probably bothering him. "At any rate, I don't want you talking about it with her. If anyone's gonna say something, it's me."

"I know. You've told me." Red's insistence on secrecy baffled Sylvia. Why couldn't the Sullivans just sit down like a normal family and hash it all through? They could have sorted out the estate years ago, even while Gran was still alive. It wasn't like she was going to live forever, as she often pointed out herself. She'd been a provocative woman who Sylvia had not always appreciated but they'd shared the same pragmatic views about life and death, and money, and now, Sylvia was losing her patience for the way the Sullivan offspring were conducting themselves.

It was rare that Sylvia squared off against Red. Usually they agreed on everything, or at least, Sylvia went along with most things because honestly, she didn't see the point of always having an opinion. She was happy with her life. She didn't need any headaches.

"I don't want to argue with you, Red." Sylvia took a plate from the cupboard and cutlery from a drawer.

"Aren't you eating?" Red asked.

"No."

"Why not?"

"I'm not hungry."

Red huffed and shook his head. Every day he acted as though Sylvia's keto diet was news to him and every day, he let her know he thought she was nuts to not be eating three square meals like regular people.

When they'd met online, of course Red hadn't known that Sylvia was an obese woman. She hadn't disguised it, but she'd posted only one blurry photo of herself and it was a headshot. They'd chatted back and forth for a couple of weeks before Red asked her to meet him for ice cream. Sylvia believed once he saw her in real life he'd run for the hills. But he hadn't. He'd told her she was pretty. And all her blubber didn't scare him off. In the past two years, by eating keto, she'd lost a hundred pounds but Red claimed he liked her better with some peanut butter and jelly under her skin.

Sylvia scraped Red's fries and fish sticks onto a plate and set it in front of him with ketchup and malt vinegar.

"How can you not be hungry?" he asked, digging in. "What'd you eat today?" Red often demanded a full accounting and no matter what Sylvia told him, he was convinced she was starving herself.

"We had a big lunch. There's new guests at the inn. An older couple—drove up from Kingston." Sylvia pulled a chair out and sat down with Red at the table. "Kaffy thought they'd be hungry when they arrived so we planned a big meal. She's going to serve them a light dinner on her own tonight."

"She won't be doing that much longer," Red said, lifting the letter from the lawyer and dropping it back on the table. "Maxine says it will sell quickly."

Sylvia had never liked Red's sister Maxine. In fact, when she met the Sullivan clan, she didn't like any of them very much: the grandmother with her blunt proclamations and needling sense of humor, Kaffy who was clearly troubled, and Maxine—so overly groomed with her perfect hair and fingernails, and so condescending. The first time they'd met, Maxine, unsolicited, had offered financial advice to Sylvia, and immediately, Sylvia didn't trust her—she was too slick and smooth. Kaffy though, Sylvia had changed her mind about, over time. She saw how Kaffy, although strange and awfully peevish, looked after her grandparents, thanklessly Sylvia would add. And she'd grown to admire Kaffy and consider her a friend.

"I don't want to talk about this, Red."

He plowed ahead. "As soon as we hesitate the clock starts ticking. You think the government's gonna wait around for their money? Capital gains and all that. We're gonna have to come up with some cash fast. How do you propose we do that?"

How convenient that Maxine was a real estate agent, filling Red's mind with these kinds of worries. Sylvia expected the plan included Maxine selling the property and making a big fat commission on top of her inheritance. Sylvia didn't know when or how but somehow Maxine had got to Red and persuaded him that it would cost him too much money to receive an inheritance. Crazy.

Red became antsy whenever they talked about money. He wasn't savvy with it. After she'd moved in with him, Sylvia had discovered he was thousands of dollars in debt to about four different credit card companies. Fortunately, he owned the house outright having paid off the mortgage for his mother before she died. His sisters had just let him keep it. It was a wonder Maxine hadn't wanted to sell it too. That was all before Sylvia's time, back when Red was a mechanic and making decent money. Later, because of his rheumatism, he'd stopped working and racked up the credit card debt like there was no tomorrow. Every time a bank offered him a new card, he'd sign on the dotted line and stopped using the old one—the trouble was, he never paid off the original one either.

Red pushed away from the table and went back to the living room. He turned up the volume on the TV—it was time for *Jeopardy.* Sylvia washed the ketchup smear off his plate and set it in the dish rack. She looked outside. It was dreary but a few hours of daylight remained.

"Don't forget about that financial planner I mentioned," Sylvia said. "Have you thought any more about talking to him?" Red ignored her and turned the volume on the TV a notch louder. He gnawed on one of his cuticles and with his other hand made a swatting motion at Sylvia to leave him alone.

With a tiny broom and dustpan Sylvia swept up the seeds from around Dickey-Bird's cage. The budgie chattered at her as he hopped from perch to perch. He was a real character, this Dickey-Bird. He was the only bird Sylvia had ever known who wanted to play with a cat—her lovable orange tabby, Hugo, who'd gone missing a couple of months ago.

Dickey-Bird agitated for Sylvia to let him out of the cage so he could swoop around the room a few times and then land on Red's head. He used to land on Hugo's head, but Red would do. Dickey-Bird seemed to know Red disliked him, or was afraid of him—it was hard to tell which.

"Don't let that bird outta there," Red warned Sylvia. She was tempted to open the tiny door in the cage but she knew she'd have to stick around to prevent the murder of the bird and she was aware that there was not much time left to get outside and take pictures before it got dark. Tomorrow would be too late—she worried all this beautiful gloom would lift overnight. Nothing worse than a clear sunny sky for taking photographs.

"We have to talk about this sometime," Sylvia said, meaning their retirement finances. Red's spending habits had improved but were still beyond their means. Every gadget that came on the market, Red wanted: an ice-making refrigerator, a fancy toilet that squirted water up your behind—every invention advertised on TV, except for a cell phone, he didn't trust them—he said big corporations were tracking you everywhere you went. Red ordered stuff, and some of it never even made it out of the box so Sylvia was sometimes able to convince him to return it. She noticed he no longer went near the laptop he'd just had to have last year. Their government pensions would start eventually, but if they wanted to live on just that income, Red needed to stop spending so darn much.

"Why did you buy another hydraulic nail gun?" Sylvia asked. A commercial jangled. Red got up from the couch with a mumble and disappeared into the kitchen. Sylvia heard him take a beer from the fridge. It popped and fizzed as he dropped himself back onto the couch. He turned the TV up louder. "I'm watching my show, Sylvia."

"I just wondered. Did you have some project in mind that required nailing?" It annoyed her—on one hand he claimed they were moving but then he went and bought a new tool as though he planned another house repair. The box with the nail gun was leaning unopened against a wall in the hallway. Sylvia couldn't help herself, she goaded him: "I thought we were moving."

Red's head jerked toward her and she regretted opening a window for him to crawl through to argue with her about moving. "We are!" he triumphed.

"We are not!"

"Jeezuz, Sylvia why not? And don't say because of that stupid cat again." Hugo had disappeared months earlier. Sylvia believed the cat had wandered off peeved because she'd tried to make him eat oysters. How was she supposed to know cats hated oysters? Sylvia concluded that Hugo was mad at her and rambled away, maybe took up residence in an old farm building or something. Every night, she went outside and called his name. She hadn't given up hope that he'd come home so she could tell him she was sorry about the oysters. She loved Hugo, her fluffy orange guy.

"You know that cat's dead, right?"

Red's face told Sylvia that he instantly regretted what had just escaped from his mouth but it crashed down on her nonetheless and tears spurted in her eyes. She turned and yanked the door open, letting it slam behind her as she stomped to her car. "Dawg, dang, dawg, darn him!" she cursed.

Chapter 2

Kaffy opened the kitchen door and Zeke flew out ahead of her into the morning, barreling past her knees and almost toppling her down the steps. Damn dog! It was May, a Tuesday, and still dark, though the sun struggled to rise beyond the stand of pine trees on the eastern hills.

Kaffy traipsed down the lane after Zeke. He was out of sight in a flash but she knew where he was headed—the forest—their usual walking place. Zeke relished all the stinky things he found there—chipmunk burrows, snake holes, mushrooms, and tufts of grass peed on by a hidden horde of animals. Kaffy appreciated the forest for the stillness, the towering trees growing around her like a cathedral, sometimes swaying, solid and ever present. The silence was her medicine.

Kaffy stopped at the mailbox, the dog still yapping at something further along the path. She rifled through the envelopes and walked on, following the sound of Zeke's bark.

One letter was from Glen Beryl, Kaffy's brother-in-law, the executor of Gran's estate. She tore open the envelope and scanned the letter—the will would be read the following week. Good. Kaffy was keen to have the will read because it contained a bombshell about which only she knew. Her brother and sister were not going to love it, but it would provide security for Kaffy for the rest of her life. And being a never-married woman in her fifties, she needed some stability. She folded the letter over and stuck it in her back pocket as she walked, remembering.

The final straw for Gran's independent living had been failing the eye test on the mandatory, over-eighty, drivers license retesting. "I'm old now. It's official. And if I can't drive myself, I'm checking out," Gran announced. Kaffy never knew whether to laugh or not at the things Gran said. Sometimes Gran took great offense if she thought she wasn't being taken seriously. One day, before moving to an old folks' home, Gran had tasked Kaffy with driving her to a lawyer's office in Whitchurch. On the way back from Whitchurch, Gran's scent of Elizabeth Arden and Pears soap filling the car, Gran had sat smiling like a cat with a songbird in its mouth. Finally, unable to keep it to herself any longer, she'd blurted out that Kaffy would be pleasantly surprised by the change she'd just made to her will. Then Gran crossed her arms over the purse in her lap, looked out the window and didn't say another word all the way home. Kaffy had understood Gran to mean that she so appreciated the way Kaffy was running the business of Sullivan House that she was leaving it to her in the will. Kaffy had blinked back tears, almost blinded as she drove. For the first time in a long time she'd felt like someone was looking out for her.

A year later, Gran died of old age. Nothing fancy, she was merely ancient. And one afternoon in the senior's home she'd simply given up the ghost when no one was around to witness it. Kaffy felt a tad uneasy about that. She hadn't wanted Gran to move and she'd tried her best to look after Gran at home, but the old woman's needs had become more than Kaffy could cope with. At first, she'd hired a nursing service to come by, but she couldn't abide the daily invasion of overly helpful nurses, each with her particular chitter-chatter and method of carrying out duties. The intrusion of guests at the inn was hard enough for Kaffy. Her nerves could stand only so many human interactions in a day.

Gran, being more social than Kaffy, had been the one to suggest the move to "The Home" as she'd called it, where she'd be meeting people and having, from Kaffy's point of view, a never ending parade of white coats barging in and out of her room, poking and jabbing her and asking intrusive questions.

Kaffy touched her hand to the folded envelope in her back pocket, reminding herself to write the lawyer's appointment into her day timer after the dog walk. It was unlikely she'd forget such an important appointment, but things often slipped her mind lately and, maybe because of menopause, her forgetfulness was worsening. If she didn't write a thing down it might as well vanish into the fog.

Zeke ran further into the forest than was usual and Kaffy trudged after him. Twenty years ago, she'd never have imagined herself living here near the forest. After residing in the city so long she'd forgotten what it was like—the quietness at night, the black sky with its dense scattering of pinprick stars, a fox sitting in a ditch scratching an itch behind its ear, a panicky pheasant dashing across the road in front of the car flapping off into the trees on the far side.

After Pops died, and it was just Kaffy and Gran, they'd started fixing things up around the inn. The place needed a coat of paint and the yard work had been neglected for several seasons. Even though Red lived right up the road, he hadn't bothered lending a hand when Pops became too frail to trim the spirea or rake up the leaves. Kaffy figured Red was only helping out now because she paid him. Money from a lawsuit had come in for Kaffy and since she was inheriting the inn anyway, she didn't mind spending a little of her settlement on Sullivan House, paying Red now and then.

Kaffy turned off the graveled path and entered the forest. Zeke was nowhere to be seen but she could hear him barking far off down the path. Morning was breaking and the trees were alive with birds singing and calling. The air smelled fresh and the pungency of the forest sprung up with each step as she crushed a thick carpet of pine needles.

In her teens, Kaffy had worked in a horse stable and in her twenties, in restaurants, often on the early shift. She remembered how much she'd resented the sound of birdsong back then, dragging herself awake to the blare of a clock-radio, rushing to work in the chilly morning air. Chirping. A chickadee-dee-dee.

In Toronto, Kaffy had lived near a church and sprawling graveyard at the corner of Woodbine and Kingston Road, and every day on her way to the streetcar stop she'd passed by an intriguing little store. Displayed in the front windows were fancy carved tombstones. Unbeknownst to Kaffy, the death-and-dying industry had been taken over by corporate interests and the hands-on stuff, such as buying coffins, selecting grave markers, and engraving marble had moved into private offices, out of the public's eye. One day, evidently, the tombstone shop had succumbed to the shift in the industry and closed up, its windows emptied of gravestones. It sat empty for nearly a year. Kaffy felt a nagging wistfulness about the forlorn little store.

Even with the steady stream of cars, trucks, and streetcars hurtling along Kingston Road, Kaffy had found the churchyard calming and reassuring. Every day she walked by noticing changes to the shrubs and hedges, to the clusters of flowers on the graves. In the spring, when the churchyard was a spray of pale blossoms from the flowering crabapple trees, Kaffy couldn't tear her eyes away.

One day, after experiencing yet another humiliation under another manager, and on a furious tear about quitting her job and starting her own business, Kaffy stormed into the church to find the priest. Surprised by her suggestion, but with pecuniary measures in mind, the Reverend had put Kaffy in touch with the church's property managers, who were only too happy to lease the store to her. And that is how The Eternity Café was born.

At the beginning, some people in the neighborhood complained that the name and location were ghoulish but Kaffy's coffee shop on the edge of the graveyard soon became a hit and a bit of a destination. Customers sat sipping their drinks while looking out the windows at the dog walkers and the moms with baby carriages who took their daily strolls along the pathways of the cemetery.

Looking back, those were the best years of Kaffy's life and she still couldn't quite believe they were over. She hadn't felt lonely back then. She'd even been able to stop taking her meds. She'd looked forward to the early mornings, sweeping the floor of the café, baking piles of muffins, and buttering up bagels that the customers ate by the dozen. Gradually, she'd invested in a fancy espresso machine, which had cost about as much as a tombstone itself. After the TV show *Friends* introduced Central Perk, coffee shops became de rigueur and with clientele at The Eternity Café already established, sales soared.

One day, an enormous billboard appeared at the corner of Woodbine and Kingston announcing an upcoming residential development. At first, Kaffy paid no attention. Condos and townhouses were popping up everywhere—even the race track had been covered over in houses, the horses and gamblers moved to the west end of the city. But one day Kaffy received notice from the church that they were terminating her lease. The entire church yard was being sold.

No one in the neighborhood could believe it could be true. Developers were planning to exhume graves and move caskets and headstones elsewhere? Presumably the deceased would be moved where land was less valuable, less desirable but some soulless enterprise was about to build houses for people to live in on the site of a cemetery.

No one called The Eternity ghoulish after that. Rather, the developers were given that descriptor. Neighborhood regulars of The Eternity Café started calling the development E-ville.

There were protests of course and Kaffy led the way. The project was a desecration, which she tried to stop with petitions and demonstrations. She didn't like to admit it but she became so consumed with the matter she was arrested eventually for leaving a dead animal on the porch of the model home. The arrest garnered a lot of publicity, with video of a harassed looking Kaffy, still in her dirty baker's apron, being arrested in handcuffs outside The Eternity. If anything, it made the public even more sympathetic toward Kaffy, and the developers looked like fiends.

With the tide of public opinion in Kaffy's favor, a lawyer presented himself one day at the Eternity and offered to help. So Kaffy sued the developer for harassment. The lawsuit and the threat of the lawsuit also attracted all kinds of press and the closing days of the Eternity were some of Kaffy's most lucrative.

One day, just before the end, Kaffy had received an offer from the developer, so unexpectedly large she'd have been a fool to refuse it. Kaffy's sister, Maxine, had dropped by. She'd been coming around quite a bit back then, which surprised Kaffy. For years, she hadn't seen or heard from Maxine. But during the fight with the developer, Maxine suddenly appeared, offering advice, and lending an ear to the endless saga.

Also, on the day of the incredible settlement offer, Maxine had delivered the news that Pops was ailing and that Gran was at her wits end—maybe Kaffy could go stay with them and let Maxine figure out what to do next? It looked like Pops would have to go into long term care.

Kaffy's lawyer encouraged her to go. Take a break. He'd squeeze a bit more out of the developers and she could look after Gran and Pops.

And that was how Kaffy's reign as the queen of the Eternity Café ended. Previously, she'd never given a thought to her future, or how she'd afford to live if something terrible happened, or if something good failed to happen. She was younger of course, but she'd felt back then as if she had everything nailed down, that nothing would fly away or disintegrate. She was stable. Who cared if she didn't have a husband? Not everyone had to have one in this world. A woman could run a business and interact with all the people she needed to in a day. More, in fact, than she could comfortably stand. Kaffy had always made her way through the world alone—it felt normal. People who couldn't were weaklings.

Although she was close to Gran as a child, Kaffy had not been a dutiful granddaughter. After her mother died and she moved to the city, she'd rarely thought about her grandparents or visited them. She'd lived those years as though she had no family. She had her life, it wasn't the greatest, but a viable alternative had never presented itself. So, when Maxine mentioned Pops was ill and Kaffy might want to drive up and check in on him and Gran, Kaffy went. It wasn't like she had anything else to do, other than fret over the demise of The Eternity Cafe.

Three years later, Kaffy was still trying not to regret the loss. At the time, Pops had been completely dependent on Gran, who had no one to look after her. Kaffy, adept at getting coffee and making muffins, was accustomed to serving bothersome customers, so it wasn't a stretch for her to take over the inn for Gran. She'd kept a trickle of money coming in while throwing meals together for Gran and Pops.

What in the world was Zeke barking at? Kaffy hoped to hell it wasn't a porcupine again. All she needed was another bill from that quack veterinarian. She hurried along the trail noticing the zillions of tiny green things that had shot up over the past couple of days. Kaffy sniffed the air—no skunk or she'd have smelled it by now.

Zeke stood, his body braced and tail aloft, barking at a large white horse. Why on earth was a horse out here alone in the forest? Kaffy drew closer. She could see the horse's head twisted at an odd angle and the horse thrashing around, moving in a semicircle, back and forth in front of Zeke who bowed and barked at it.

"Shush now." Kaffy waved Zeke away.

A hefty old birch tree was down, freshly broken—fallen in the storm the day before. The birch lay across a wire fence that Kaffy had never noticed before. The forest was on Gran's property but Kaffy wasn't aware of where it started and stopped. The rusty fence marked an unnecessary boundary, she knew that much. The nearest neighbor was the horse ranch up the highway. When she was young, Kaffy had worked there as a stable-hand. A woman named Gwen operated it now, renting out horses for trail rides through the forest. The white horse was probably one of hers.

The horse's halter was snagged on a broken piece of wire fencing and she was frightened, her eye wild and white as Kaffy approached.

Then Kaffy spied a foal. It couldn't have been more than a few days old—still fuzzy around the forehead and as innocent a creature as Kaffy had ever seen. The foal stood behind its mother, several feet into the thicker bushes but the mare couldn't see the baby and Kaffy guessed that was part of the reason she was so frantic. "Settle down, now," she said, hoping to soothe the mare as she approached. "I'm not going to hurt you or your baby. Let me just see what's happening here."

The mare snorted and shook her head back and forth trying to free herself. Kaffy could see that the entrapment wasn't complicated. A wire stuck straight down. If the mare relaxed and lowered her head, she'd slip loose, but she was too agitated and tense. How long had she been trapped this way?

Between Kaffy and the mare was a broken branch. If the horse should manage to swing around and aim her powerful hooves at her, Kaffy would be somewhat protected. She ventured closer, close enough to touch the horse, speaking in a low tone. She stroked the horse's nose and the beast huffed. Kaffy could feel the strength of the mare's head and neck as she reached up to grasp its halter. She tried bending the fencing to get at the broken part but the horse nodded fiercely. Kaffy struggled with one hand to hold onto the halter while pulling at the fencing with the other. Zeke barked. The mare reared up, the fencing wrenched downward releasing the horse and at the same time catching Kaffy's finger and tearing it open. Kaffy squawked as pain resonated deep within her hand, as though the wire had hit a nerve. She bent over in agony, gasping and moaning until the throbbing subsided. A thin trickle of blood ran down her wrist. Kaffy tried not to howl as she dug with her other hand into every pocket she could reach until her fingers discovered a crumpled tissue. With some difficulty she wrapped the tissue around the injury and held it tightly to her chest to stop the bleeding and the pain. Damn it. Damn it. Stupid horse!

The freed mare nuzzled her foal, checking it over. The foal however was watching Zeke as he dashed around in a wide excited circle. The colt's coat was charcoal. It stood on awkward stilt-like legs. When it moved it appeared to jump from spot to spot. Kaffy's hostility toward the situation melted a fraction. The foal's adorability was impossible to resist. A memory popped into Kaffy's mind. She'd badly wanted a horse when she was a girl. It had driven her to distraction.

She hadn't thought of that in years.

Kaffy's family wasn't the type to get horses for their daughters. They couldn't even afford riding lessons so Kaffy worked at the stable in exchange for lessons from the rancher.

Horses had been Kaffy's endless fantasy she remembered now. Riding out in fields of wildflowers, her hair and the horse's mane flowing in the wind like she'd seen in menstruation commercials—birdbrain stuff she'd spent too much time musing on, and would've been ridiculed about endlessly if she'd confided to anyone.

The mare was large and powerful. Kaffy couldn't now imagine climbing onto a horse this size. How had she ever had the nerve? She supposed when you're around them all the time they become accustomed to you and then it feels natural to climb onto a horse's back. She eyed the foal. That would be something: a horse to ride, on these morning walks with Zeke.

Kaffy scoffed at her own nonsense.

The mare, finished with her inspection of the foal, began to graze hungrily, nibbling on the sparse blades of grass at the base of a tree. Kaffy stood watching for several minutes. Thinking about whether it would be possible to get close enough to the foal to separate it from its mother. She could take it home, keep it to herself, raise it, ride it. The urge to get close and touch its coat was overpowering.

A secondary, more rational thought rose to the surface of Kaffy's mind—she ought to do something responsible about the horses. A mare couldn't be expected to find her way back to the ranch safely, could she? But what was Kaffy supposed to do about a lost horse? She had pressing things to do today. For example, there was the email she'd received the night before from *The Lonely Tripper* moving the reservation for their reviewer up two weeks. It was imminent and the review was a big deal. Sylvia had encouraged Kaffy to invite the magazine to send a reviewer to increase reservations. *The Lonely Tripper* was distributed in hotels and airports and even went in the seat backs of one of the airlines. Sylvia showed Kaffy their social media account—photos of places all around the country. They'd even used one of Sylvia's photos, which she was excited about. She told Kaffy it gleaned four thousand likes, or something. Kaffy didn't do social media stuff like Sylvia.

The mare lifted her tail and a few rolls of brown dung fell to the floor of the forest.

Kaffy needed to get back to the inn but a crazy desire for the baby horse rippled through her. There was so much that needed doing in two weeks before the reviewer arrived. But Kaffy badly wanted that foal. She peered at it closely. Its eyes looked almost violet.

"Go on!" Kaffy cried, waving her arms at the mare. Ouch, that hurt. Kaffy's finger throbbed. She rewound the tissue and held her fist tightly. The horses stared at her, the mare still chewing, her jaw moving sideways. "Go on," Kaffy urged. "Don't you want to get back to your barn?"

That was absurd. Now that the horse had its freedom, why would it want to go back to captivity? If it hadn't got caught on the fence, it would've been free to wander wherever it wanted. The rancher was probably looking for her horse, especially a pregnant one. Maybe Kaffy should just go back to the inn, call the rancher, and tell her she'd found the horses. But she wanted that baby. She would take such good care of it.

The mare returned to grazing but the foal stared at Kaffy from its dark purple eyes. Its eyelashes and ears captivated her. Kaffy made a smooching noise with her mouth and both horses looked at her. The mare stopped eating.

"C'mere," Kaffy said to the foal. She wanted to pet it. Was its coat as soft as it looked?

The mare's ears pricked forward but she stood where she was.

Kaffy held her hand out to the foal and the mare's eyes went instantly to the tissue wrapped around Kaffy's finger, mistaking it for food. She took a step forward. Kaffy withdrew her hand. The mare stopped.

Kaffy reached out her left hand.

With eyes on Kaffy's outstretched hand the mare again walked slowly over until she placed her whiskered nostrils in Kaffy's palm and snuffled. Kaffy didn't know what to do. The horse's placidity made Kaffy think that she might not fare so well on her own. There were bears and wolves in the forest. But Kaffy couldn't walk all the way through the forest with these horses, could she? She didn't even know where the trail began. Damn it, this was annoying on a morning when she had so much to do.

Kaffy climbed gingerly over the thin metal fence between herself and the horses. The mare went back to grazing. The foal stood its ground staring at both Kaffy and Zeke in turn, curiosity overcoming its fear. The mare paid no attention as Kaffy approached the foal. She reached out and stroked the foal's head above its eyes. She interlaced her fingers through the foal's mane and tugged as she moved backwards toward the fence. When the foal took a step the mare's head came up and she stood watching, her ears pitched forward, her jaw still rhythmically munching sideways.

Kaffy stepped onto the wire fence to pin it to the ground and then coaxed the foal over it. The mare took a step toward them and Kaffy let the metal fence spring back up. Now, she had the baby all to herself. She would just lead it away. But the mare let out a wild cry and every hair on Kaffy's body stood on end. Zeke cowered on the ground. The foal thrashed, twisting out of the grasp of Kaffy's fingers in the process. Kaffy leapt back and the foal danced toward the fence. The mare paced on the other side snorting heavily, eyeing Kaffy with a murderous glare.

Kaffy's heart pounded. How stupid. She wasn't going to separate a mother from her baby.

"Easy now," she said. Zeke rushed around, not barking, but agitated. The forest seemed to be holding its breath. Kaffy squeezed her way between the foal and the wire fence. She could feel the warmth radiating from the mare's flank. "Easy, easy," she said, stepping down on the wire, flattening it against the ground. Zeke barked and the mare stepped over, knocking Kaffy with her shoulder. Kaffy fell and rolled away to avoid the commotion of hooves.

Now both horses were on Kaffy's side of the fence. Quickly she ran through her options. The first was to leave the horses right where they were. But when she looked at the foal, she imagined how an enduring affection might grow between them. Zeke's dogged loyalty was not enough. Second choice was to bring both horses back to the inn and take care of them. Would anyone notice? She didn't know what she'd do with the mare once the baby was grown but she brushed aside that consideration. Third choice, she could do the sane thing, lead the two lost horses back to Sullivan House, call their owner, and return them. Kaffy didn't have time for the madness her mind was conjuring, promising her love from a four-hoofed animal. Ridiculous.

Kaffy made the smoochy sound again until she caught the mare's attention. She held out the hand with the bandage. The mare took a step toward her. "C'mon," Kaffy said, turning toward the inn. "Come on if you're coming. I've got work to do." She began walking and to her relief the horse stepped in behind. Kaffy walked at a steady pace, the horses following. She didn't think the mare would be so obedient, but maybe the horse thought Kaffy knew what she was doing, seeing as Kaffy, a human, had just freed the animal. The foal followed its mother. Zeke, seeming pleased, ran off down the road like he'd saved the day.

Kaffy began to hum and then to sing out loud as they walked, "The old gray mare she ain't what she used to be, ain't what she used to be, ain't what she used to be. No, the old gray mare she ain't what she used to be many long years ago."

There was a brick shed at the back of the inn property. Kaffy couldn't remember the last time she'd been inside the small building. No one went in there anymore. There was no reason to since Pops had built a more conveniently located garage closer to the house. At one time, however, before Pop's Volvo, the brick shed had been a horse stable.

Dim light streaked in through a single dirty window at the back of a box stall. The horses followed Kaffy inside as though it was the most ordinary thing in the world. Her hands trembled as she closed the door to the stall. Amid the faint odor of stuffy engine oil was an even fainter smell of leather and possibly horse manure. It was a familiar scent, which unsettled Kaffy further. She searched in her pockets for another tissue and wound it around her finger, keeping her hand in a fist to hold it in place while she hunted through rusty junk at the back of the shed. She dragged a dusty bale of straw into the stall and did her best to kick the dry crackly stuff loose.

Water. They were going to need water. She'd seen a dinged-up bucket in the back of the shed. Rats, it was rusted through with a hole. And she needed to get some hay. The foal was already nursing. The mare stood in the stall, staring past Kaffy.

Chapter 3

The phone was ringing.

Red roused himself, tossing the covers aside, and stumbled into the living room to answer it. He'd been aware, throughout a fitful night, that Sylvia had not come home. Now, rushing for the phone, he was desperate to hear her voice. He knew he'd messed up by mentioning Hugo's inevitable death.

"Hey there, lover boy." It was his sister.

Maxine had taken to teasing Red ever since the laptop fiasco. Red fumed, but what could he say? He was indebted to Maxine in a way no one could ever find out about. He scrunched his face in frustration and held a shallow breath. "Hey, Maxine," he said through gritted teeth.

Maxine wondered if Red had received the letter from her husband, Glen about the reading of the will. "This is our big moment," she said. "We're going to be rich."

Red's stomach panged. Getting rich by selling Gran and Pop's property had never been part of any plan he'd hatched over the years. When he bought the laptop, he'd had notions of upgrading his education, learning new skills. He couldn't work on cars anymore because of arthritis and he couldn't be Kaffy's handyman for the rest of his life—he'd only started helping out because he got to keep an eye on Sylvia. He needed to find a different way to earn money and he'd seen on television something that led him to believe he could make a living online from the privacy of his own home. He'd jumped on the idea, which had all gone to crap.

Maxine yammered on about the timeline for selling the property and the division of the assets. "And then you can pay me back the money you owe me and neither of us will mention any of that ever again," she finished, sealing the deal on Red's guilty conscience. He'd been forced to ask Maxine for help. Actually, she'd guessed he was in some kind of trouble and had cajoled him into confiding in her. Fortunately, and somewhat surprisingly, she'd known exactly what to do, and she'd helped him. She took over the whole sordid affair and fixed it.

The laptop rested on a shelf across the room like a dangerous snapping turtle, dormant now perhaps, but ready to bite off his fingers should Red dare to prod it back to life. He hung up the phone and shuffled into the kitchen. He'd slept terribly, which wasn't unusual these days. Ever since the cursed email had arrived six months ago, he'd been restless as heck. Red would fall to sleep like a dead man but then wake up with a start in the middle of the night, Sylvia sleeping soundly at his side. His brain would then start replaying the whole mess he'd made of his life and he'd squirm around in the sheets until the birds started tweeting.

From: Dom Vitkus dvitkusppd@onlook.com

Subject line: ReDS777

Red remembered the zap of shock he'd felt when he'd read his own clever password in the subject line of an email. His eyes scanned the message, his heartbeat quickening and his hands turned into two cold dead fish at the ends of his arms.

Do you think it was some joke or that you can ignore me? I see what you are doing. Stop shopping and screwing around, your time is almost over. Yea, I know what you were doing the past couple of days. I have been observing your activities.

Red's eyes watered. He'd been browsing online when photos of pretty girls had popped up. Nothing dirty, just women with nice long hair, snug fitting if not scanty clothing, and something inside Red stirred. Without thinking about it, he'd clicked.

By the way, a nice car you have got there. I wonder how it will look with the pics of your dick and face.

His car? What did those girly websites have to do with his car? Did they mean Sylvia's car? And what did it mean, *pics of his dick?*

Since you ignored my last email and disregarded me, I am posting the videos I recorded of you masturbating to the porn right now.

Red almost passed out.

I will upload the videos along with some of your details to the online forum.

What forum?

Panic rushed through Red's being like a cold frothy river. He'd seen the word 'forum' before but it wasn't anything he was familiar with.

I am sure they will love to see you in action, and you will soon discover what is going to happen to you.

They? Who's they?

If you do not fund this bitcoin address with $5000 within the next two days, I will contact your relatives and everybody on your contact lists and show them your recordings.

Oh, no! That they.

Send: $5000 to this Bitcoin address: 16DM25kkuds8gt8kM9WuYPBTJ5sN3sqypk

Red's brain scrambled to make sense of the email. Drenched in shame, his heartbeat drowned out any common sense any part of him may have been whispering.

There are many places you can buy Bitstamp, Coinbase, Kraken, etc., or you can Google to find more.

What??!

If you want to save yourself - better act fast because right now you are FUCKED, we will not leave you alone, and there are many people on the groups that will make your life feel terrible.

In his panic, Red hadn't understood what the entirety of the email meant but he knew it referred to a couple of days earlier when he'd been looking at a pretty-girl video and a chat box had popped up on his screen with an invitation for him to show the woman on the other side of the camera his penis, which he was mortified to admit was in his hand at that moment. He slammed the laptop shut. Then wondered if the chat box was still there. How was he going to get it off the screen without starting the computer again? He'd zipped his pants quickly and with shaking hands lifted the lid on the laptop like peeking into a vat of snakes. The chat box was still active but Red hurriedly moused to the x in the corner of it and thank you Jesus it disappeared. Then he closed the browser and swore he would never ever click on one of those pictures again.

A day later, the email arrived.

Red poured the dusty remains of a cereal box into a bowl. He'd have to remind Sylvia to get more. He took a milk carton from the fridge and shook it. They would need milk too.

Miserably, Red wondered where Sylvia was. He knew she was fed up with his mood. They'd been squabbling a lot lately. He wanted it to stop but he was so dang edgy. Sylvia had gone off in huffs before but he'd deceived himself into believing that the way she reacted to his orneriness was healthy. Wasn't it better to go blow off some steam before saying something unforgivable?

You know that cat's dead, right?

He'd said it.

And now there was something else to add to his dungeon of regrets. The words had escaped in an irrational moment of feeling bulletproof.

Sylvia loved that cat. Very likely more than she loved him at the moment.

Red knew what to do. He'd call her. She was probably awake by now, at her Mom's house or a friend's. He'd phone and apologize and make plans with her for later. Maybe they'd order takeout food for dinner tonight or something special like that.

Red slurped up the end of the milk in his bowl and wiped his chin on the shoulder of his t-shirt. He walked into the living room to use the phone, hopeful that Sylvia would forgive him. She always had before. She seemed to have unending patience for his worst characteristics.

Red punched in Sylvia's phone number and across the living room a dog started barking. Red jumped and spun. Sylvia's phone, on the table beside her favorite chair, was lit up. Barking. Pressed to his ear, the house phone continued to call. Sylvia hadn't taken her phone. She'd been so angry at him she hadn't bothered to gather her things when she left. He'd screwed things up bad this time.

Red hung up the phone and the barking stopped. He went over to the end table and picked up Sylvia's phone. It was hard and cold and the screen was black in his hand. She'd programmed their home number to sound like a dog barking. That's what Sylvia thought of him. Red lay the phone face down on the table.

Chapter 4

Red was in the driveway by his truck when Kaffy emerged from the stable. Her heart stopped. Damn him, he always showed up at the most inconvenient times. Actually, there was no good time to have Red around. Kaffy shut the shed door, her trembling hands fiddling the archaic latch into place.

Red squinted at Kaffy. "What're you doing in *there*?" He took a quick drag on his vape. It was his newest acquisition and he looked like an idiot.

"Nothing," she lied. Her mind scrambled to assess the situation from Red's point of view. Was an explanation necessary? No, it was her shed—she could be inside it if she wanted to be. Well, it wasn't technically *her* shed, yet, but she lived at the inn, and Red didn't. Squatter's rights.

Red's current project was fixing the porch. He'd begun last year in the fall and he was still working on it now in mid-May. His pace drove Kaffy up the wall. He knew very well the busy season was coming, and yet he moved like a snail. Sullivan Place needed that porch for the view it afforded of the river.

Decades ago, when Gran and Pops had opened the inn there'd been a clear river just across the road, with a dock for swimming and boats for short trips into the forest and down river to fish. As everywhere these days, the water now was too polluted to swim in and its depth too unpredictable to boat on. No one would dare eat a fish from the river, if they managed to catch one, but it remained pretty to look at. Someday, Kaffy hoped, someone in government would come to their senses and clean up the river, restore it to its natural state. Gran had wanted the pollution stopped at its source—she'd been a true conservationist. As it was, guests contented themselves with sitting on the porch watching the river—that is, when there was a porch.

Kaffy skirted the driveway where Red stood and headed for the house. She hid her injured hand so he wouldn't ask about the tissue wound around her finger.

"I guess you got this?" Red pulled an envelope from his jacket pocket. It looked the same as the one she received that morning about the will still folded up in the back pocket of her jeans. With the horses and everything, she'd forgot all about it. Red took another deep draw on his vape and blew a cloud of mist from his mouth. "Kinda sad, isn't it?"

Kaffy paused. "What do you mean?"

Red never said what he meant. He always stammered and stumbled for words and never seemed to comprehend what Kaffy said to him—he'd make his mouth into an O-shape and cock his head to one side like an imbecile. Kaffy couldn't tell if he was drug addled or stupid.

"We might as well face it," Red said. "The property's gotta be split three ways." He paused and glanced down at the ground so Kaffy knew that what he said next would be a lie. "Now, I don't care one way or another but Maxine's gonna want her share."

This definitely was not true. Maxine couldn't care less about the inn and she didn't need the money. Maxine and Glen lived with their kids on a vineyard in Niagara. They took winter vacations in the Caribbean and traveled to Europe every summer. Kaffy hadn't seen any of them in—she didn't know how long. Once she settled into Sullivan House permanently, her sister had dropped out of her life just as suddenly as she'd popped into it at The Eternity Café. Maxine seemed to have no use for Kaffy, or Red, or anything to do with the inn. Kaffy didn't think Maxine had even visited Gran when she moved into The Home.

Red was referring to his own desperation for money. Sylvia had divulged to Kaffy Red's debts and the way he spent money on this and that, always ordering online or over the phone like money grew on trees. Kaffy brushed off Red's insinuation that Maxine wanted her share. Anyway, once the will was read, it wouldn't matter. On top of everything else, Kaffy held a suspicion that Gran hadn't liked Red or Maxine all that much. She wouldn't be surprised if Gran left them nothing at all. It would serve Red right. Kaffy set her mouth and turned away. She knew she alone would inherit the inn but she couldn't tell Red what she knew. He'd accuse her of influencing Gran behind his back. He'd always thought the worst of her.

Kaffy climbed the back steps to the kitchen door leaving Red in the driveway. She refused to fall into the trap of arguing with him. She needed to stay focused on fixing up the inn in time for *The Lonely Tripper* reviewer. She pulled the letter and envelope from her back pocket. She needed to find her day-timer to write in the appointment for the reading of the will.

Kaffy washed her injured finger in the kitchen sink and watched Red through the window. There was no reason for him to, but it would surprise Kaffy if he didn't go snooping around the old brick stable having seen her come out the door.

Instead, Red disappeared into the chicken coop. One of the tasks he took care of around Sullivan House was emptying the rat trap under the hen house. Every now and then there was an invasion of the loathsome creatures. Red was handy for some things.

After she washed the dried blood off, Kaffy could hardly see the cut on her finger, as though it had swallowed itself up. There was only a small round mark, which hurt like a chainsaw wound when she touched it. Kaffy dried her hands and went to the bathroom in search of a bandage. Force of habit, she adjusted a crooked frame in the hall as she passed. Everything needed to be just so for the guests.

The wall running alongside the staircase displayed a row of Sylvia's framed photographs. Every now and then a guest bought one, which served to encourage Sylvia, creating more places to dust and more picture frames to keep straight. Sylvia's subject matter was melancholy but Kaffy admitted they were eerily beautiful. Sylvia gushed on and on about capturing the light on dismal days, or right after it rained when everything was wet and dripping, not unlike the weather they'd been having lately. It was a rainy, cold spring, the kind of weather that put Kaffy in a worse mood than usual.

She checked every drawer in the bathroom but found no bandages. Where was the first-aid kit? Sylvia had it out all the time. She was always hurting herself in the kitchen—cutting her thumb on the potato peeler or grating the skin off her knuckles into the carrots. Sylvia would be arriving to work soon and she'd know where the bandages were. Kaffy wrapped some toilet paper around her finger in the meantime.

Kaffy had expected to dislike Sylvia. Why a sane woman would marry Red Sullivan, she could never figure out. So, originally, she hadn't paid any attention to Sylvia. But then Gran got sick and Sylvia started coming around and offering to help. At first, Kaffy regarded everything Sylvia did as a nuisance—a bit too nice, a little too interfering. Didn't she have enough to do looking after Red? But Sylvia had no children and Red was home all the time having packed in working in the garage. Maybe Sylvia needed to get away from him. Kaffy had heard that story many times from women back in the days of The Eternity Cafe. Husbands retired and wives immediately went out and found jobs.

Sylvia had started coming by every day to help out, and Sullivan House began to look attractive and inviting. Without Gran telling Kaffy she shouldn't do this and she better not do that, Sylvia and Kaffy added dishes to the menu, and moved the furniture around—sometimes right out the door into the back of Red's truck and straight to the garbage dump.

After Gran moved to The Home, Kaffy decided there was no reason to leave Sullivan House, no need to move back to the city or find somewhere else to live. The old house had become her home and when the inn began to turn a profit, Kaffy started paying Sylvia for her work, and even threw a few dollars at Red now and then even though he should have been working for free, like Kaffy had the past few years.

When the Eternity Café closed, Kaffy had been forced to think about how she would finance the rest of her life. Working for somebody else was out of the question. She refused. Never again. But she also knew how hard it was to start a business. An established one, like Sullivan House, was invaluable, so why not try making into a going-concern again? The inn had been long established, and with the ease of online bookings, bed and breakfasts were more popular all the time.

Sullivan House was in an ideal location—close to Toronto, but once guests arrived, they were far enough away to forget all about the city. Sure, the highway was just two lanes but at least it was a highway. And it was only twenty minutes or so to the expressway that ran straight to Toronto.

Winter or summer, nothing compared to the views of the forest from every window of Sullivan House. Woodland creatures appeared and disappeared—deer, hawks, rabbits, fox. And guests loved snapping photos of them. Sylvia started social media for Sullivan House and posted pictures that seemingly garnered some attention. She told Kaffy that guests consistently tagged the inn, whatever that meant. And in addition to forgetting about their horrible jobs in the city and gorging on food they didn't have to cook themselves, there was a lot for guests to do around Sullivan House. In the winter they could ski on groomed trails through the forest. Kaffy didn't allow snowmobiles on the inn's property but up the road were the horse trails where skidooers blasted through the woods in the winter. Sometimes Kaffy even liked the sound of them in the distance. In summer, trail rides were the attraction. It seemed everyone wanted to ride a horse once in their lifetime.

No, Sullivan House was the perfect source of income for Kaffy. She would live here for the rest of her life as her grandmother had. Gran would've wanted her to carry on the tradition. She hadn't poured her entire life into the place to watch it vanish overnight.

Where was Sylvia? It wasn't like her to be late for work. Kaffy heard the guests stirring upstairs—it was just one couple currently. Soon they'd be down looking for their breakfasts. Kaffy carried a pot of fresh coffee into the dining room and turned on the hot plate then went back to the kitchen to lay some strips of bacon in the frying pan. She took a cranberry loaf from the fridge.

"Red, where's Sylvia?" Kaffy called to her brother from the back door of the inn.

Red shrugged. He fiddled with the tailgate of his truck. Infuriating—he was always tinkering and fidgeting.

"Isn't she coming to work today?"

Red looked at Kaffy, his face expressionless but somewhat grim. "I haven't seen her." What did he mean by that, he got out of bed earlier than she did?

"Is she sick or something?"

Again, Red shrugged.

The tailgate flopped open and hit him in the chest. "Son of a gun!"

Hearing the guests behind her in the dining room, Kaffy hurried back inside to attend to them. Fortunately, they were happy with bacon and coffee and were already buttering pieces of cranberry loaf. They were a spunky older couple who wanted to know all the things they could do during their stay, so Kaffy, hiding her wrapped finger, gave them the usual spiel about hiking trails and the pretty manmade lake nearby where you could sometimes catch a fish, and the observatory at the top of the moraine, and the trail-horse ranch up the highway.

Kaffy's stomach clenched as she remembered the horses in the shed. What a bird-brained thing she'd gone and done, luring them down to the inn and secreting them away. But she'd done it now and there was no undoing it.

"It must be nice here in the winter," the woman said.

"Hm? Oh, yes. There's cross country skiing and skating..." The guests smiled at each other. Kaffy wondered if they weren't a bit doddering to be participating in winter sports.

It was maddening that Sylvia hadn't shown up yet for work. She'd be so excited when she heard the reservation from *The Lonely Tripper* was now imminent. And with the reviewer coming—they needed to get ready even faster than before. It was now crucial that Red get the porch finished before the review. Sylvia planned to paint some of the porch rockers—that seemed like a must-do now. And there was menu planning, and how was their stock of wine? Damn it, they hadn't even finished the spring cleaning.

Red unloaded tools from the back of his truck.

"Are you working on the porch today?" Anxiety coursed through Kaffy's chest and it caused her question to come out more shrewish than she'd intended. She instantly regretted her direct approach. She'd learned to be careful how she spoke to Red. She never knew when he would turn on her and bark. Her nerves couldn't take it.

Red paused, midway from lifting a tool box. "I thought I'd get at it, yea." He stared at Kaffy, wasting time—the man couldn't multitask if his life depended on it. "Why? You got something you'd rather me do?"

"No, no, that's fine," Kaffy answered, backing off. She'd already decided against telling him about the reviewer. He'd just ridicule it, or worse, stop working and sabotage the whole thing. He couldn't be trusted. "I'm just wondering where Sylvia is?"

Red frowned. "I told you, I don't know." He trudged toward the porch. He'd already torn off the floorboards and repaired the corner columns, which were rotting around the base. It was a bigger job than Kaffy had anticipated. She'd asked Red to replace a few boards but once he got going, he'd warned her that the condition of the wood was a lot worse than she'd thought.

"Have you picked up the wood for the floor?" Kaffy followed him. She knew her questions risked pushing Red into suspicion. She rarely spoke to him, she just left him to his work. Sylvia was their go-between. Now Red would wonder why Kaffy was pestering him, and start firing back questions of his own. But he just said, "Not yet."

The guests appeared around the side of the house and stopped to find out what was happening with the porch and wasn't Red all friendly and full of answers. Kaffy wished they'd go away and leave the lout to get his work done.

"It must be nice here in the summer," the woman mused, taking in the view afforded from that side of the house. It faced the forest and the rise of the moraine. The porch was open on three sides and in the summer the sun warmed the southeast end, swung around the back of the house then reappeared in the afternoon at the other end. Surrounding the inn maples towered shielding the porch from the glaring afternoon sun. They weren't fully in leaf yet. In the evening the porch offered a spectacular view of the sun setting into the hill of pine and spruce, the sky turning scarlet, tangerine then violet.

"You'll have to come back in the hotter weather," Kaffy said. She'd been learning from Sylvia how to be a gracious host. She'd never believed in kissing up to people but Sylvia claimed that repeat clientele was the most important asset the inn could possess. She'd taken a hospitality course over the internet at some point in her life when she was trying to figure out a career.

"We're going to try to get up to the observatory," the man told Kaffy. "We'll see you later."

Kaffy waved her uninjured hand as the couple's car exited the driveway.

...

Kaffy checked the long-term weather forecast. Cold wet weather—unusual for May, and it had been a brutally long winter. Normally, by this time of year, small leaves covered the trees, some even flowering, but this spring everything was slow to bud. As a result, the inn would need firewood, and lots of it, to take the chill off in the mornings. Kaffy might even need to order another cord, unless there was some out by the shed.

The shed. Damn, she'd forgotten about the horses again. She needed to get out there and see about getting them some water. Grass was scant around the inn just yet, and Kaffy couldn't very well let the mare out to graze, someone would see her. She needed to get her hands on some hay somehow. She thought of the farms in the area that had giant rolls of hay sitting in their fields in the summer. Surely, one of them would sell her some. There was a tack shop up the highway. They'd know where she could buy hay.

Red was still outside.

She needed a bandage.

Kaffy phoned Red's number—the one for his and Sylvia's house phone. Red insisted on keeping a landline. He didn't trust cell phones—anybody could listen in, he claimed. Plus, they gave you brain cancer.

The phone in Red's house, Kaffy pictured it in the living room on the end table beside the couch where it had been since she was a child, rang and rang until the answering machine picked up. No voice mail service for Red—he didn't need Ma Bell listening in on all his messages. Kaffy spoke into the machine. "Sylvia? Are you there? Call me." She hung up. Her finger throbbed. She flicked through her recent contacts and called Sylvia's cell phone. It went immediately to voicemail, which meant Sylvia was on the line or her phone was off. Kaffy left another message. And texted, "Are you coming today?"

There was a great deal of work to do to get ready for the reviewer and Kaffy was counting on Sylvia to help out, even more so now with her cut finger. Sylvia worked hard and diligently and she went along with things Kaffy proposed. Plus, she'd be excited about the reviewer, and Kaffy hated to admit it but Sylvia's enthusiasm was almost as important to Kaffy as her muscle.

Kaffy took out a notepad and started making plans for the menu for the weekend of the review. Everything needed to be perfect. She made lists of what she would need to shop for and what she could make herself or get Sylvia to make. Wine. What wines would go with the meals? How many bottles?

The inn had three reservations already for that weekend. In which room would she put the reviewer in? Kaffy mulled over the bedrooms on the second floor. Some afforded better views than others, some were cozier. Two had fireplaces. One was spacious and had a king-size bed.

A crash jolted Kaffy out of her musing. She rushed to the living room to find Red throwing pieces of wood into the box next to the fireplace. "It's gonna be cold for the next while," he said. "You're gonna need more wood. There's none left by the shed."

He'd been back to the shed? Had he heard the horses? Had he poked his nosy nose inside and seen them? Kaffy's palms broke into a sweat.

Chips of wood lay scattered over the rug. Darn it. Where was Sylvia? Kaffy grabbed the broom and started sweeping bits and pieces furiously into the hearth. Her finger throbbed. Red stomped past her. "One more load for now," he said. Kaffy waited, annoyed, but also anxious about the horses and Red discovering them. In a minute or two Red stomped back in with another armload of wood. Again, it thundered onto the floor and he began hurling pieces into the box.

"Must you throw it down like that?"

Red looked over his shoulder at Kaffy, his pale eyebrows raised. It appeared that Kaffy was criticizing him—it shocked her too. Usually, she avoided any kind of conflict with Red. Today was stressing her out!

"Where *is* Sylvia?" she asked again, deflecting from the stew of anxiety and annoyance brewing inside her. What had happened to her dependable sister-in-law?

Kaffy's persistence seemed to infuriate Red. "I already told you I don't know!"

Kaffy breathed a few times then prodded, "Well, when was the last time you saw her?" She tried to make her voice sound helpful like she was trying to assist Red in locating his lost keys or a wallet, but this time it was his wife. Red scowled and went back to shuffling the wood around in the box. "Come on, Red," Kaffy pleaded. The floor was a mess of wood chips and broken bark. "There's stuff to do around here that needs doing, and I'm just wondering when she's going to get here!" Red stopped and with his back to Kaffy said, "We had a fight last night, okay?"

Oh.

But what did that have to do with Sylvia's whereabouts now?

"I haven't seen her since then," Red finished, his shoulders tense. He stood absolutely still, a piece of firewood in each hand.

"You mean she didn't sleep in her own bed last night?" Kaffy asked tentatively. "Red turned and eyeballed her, breathing forcefully through his nose, his face redder than usual, his pale eyes watery. "Maybe she went off to her mother's. I don't know. She took off."

Kaffy suspected Red controlled Sylvia's friendships and even her relationship with her family. Sylvia talked about Red affectionately, as if it was sweet that Red was overprotective, and amazingly she never complained about him. But Kaffy sensed a weird tension between the two of them, especially over the past few months, however she couldn't remember them ever having a fight, not one so bad that Sylvia went home to her mother's. In fact, Kaffy couldn't recall Sylvia ever visiting her family outside of the holidays.

Red brushed past Kaffy, the door shutting hard behind him. She heard the engine of his truck fire up and the gravel crunching on the driveway as he pulled away from the inn.

...

The young gal at the desk in the tack shop was more concerned with getting back to her phone than asking any follow up questions to Kaffy's initial inquiry about hay. No, they didn't sell it. No, she didn't know where Kaffy could get any. Kaffy paid with cash for a water bucket and slipped out of the store with as little fuss as possible. The horses would remain a secret, for now.

Instead of heading toward home, she drove further up the highway to a sideroad where she presumed there would be farms. Traveling along, she soon spied a place with a sign near the mailbox, *Fresh Eggs for Sale*. At least it was a farm in the business of dealing with people who just dropped by. Kaffy drove down the driveway between two fields, past the farmhouse to a small parking area. She got out of the car and looked around. The place was deserted except for the cattle on the far side of the field.

A screen door slammed and a woman emerged from the farmhouse with a carton of eggs in each hand. "Hi there. You looking for eggs?" Kaffy shook her head, no, and approached. "Actually, I'm in the market for a bale of hay."

The woman stared at her. "We don't sell hay."

"I know, but I mean, I'd like to buy some hay from you, if you have it, for the cows I mean." The woman regarded Kaffy skeptically. "We don't sell hay," she repeated, enunciating each word. An exasperating woman—where was the farmer? He'd know what Kaffy meant.

"I just need a bale of hay. Could you ask your husband?"

The woman's face scorched red and her eyes flared. "My husband? My husband? Who do you think you are coming around here asking about my husband?"

Kaffy backed away towards her car. "I'm sorry, I didn't mean . . ." She'd hit a nerve. The woman looked like she was about to start pelting Kaffy's car with eggs.

Kaffy gunned the engine and sped down the driveway, her arms trembling as she drove. Her finger throbbed. She didn't know if she could persevere.

Further down the road, another farm, a pinch shabbier, appeared. Kaffy was relieved to find an old man in overalls and a trucker's cap back behind the house tinkering with a tractor. He'd know what she was talking about.

Kaffy made her request and the farmer pushed back his hat and scratched his forehead. "Now what in the world would you need a bale of hay for?"

Kaffy was ready for this. She'd concocted a story on the way. "I'm a teacher," she tossed off. "And I'm having a donkey visit our school. I thought it would be nice to have some hay for him to eat."

A divot appeared between the farmer's eyebrows and he looked at Kaffy with the same suspicion and judgment she'd received at the previous farm. Why were these farmers hoarding their hay? They were so unfriendly. The old man didn't say anything for a long time—just puckered his mouth and appeared to be thinking. Finally, he turned and headed for the barn. "Twenty bucks," he said over his shoulder.

Kaffy expelled the breath she'd been holding. At least she now had a business arrangement. When she needed more, she would come back.

...

The mare nickered shrilly, as if to let Kaffy know she was outraged when Kaffy entered the stable. "Shhh," Kaffy hushed but the horse stamped her hoof. She must have been extremely thirsty and hungry. What kind of a person believes she can take in a horse and a foal like a stray cat with a kitten, Kaffy scolded herself.

With a rusted tool she tried sawing through the twine on the bale of hay but the cut on her right hand made gripping the implement painful. The mare kicked at the stall wall and a jolt of adrenaline blasted through Kaffy's body. After a few panicked sawing motions, the twine broke and the hay bale fell apart while Kaffy kicked at it. The mare snorted when the first few handfuls of hay came over the stall door. Kaffy couldn't recall how much a horse would eat in a day. She peered through the bars in the stall door and watched the foal. He was such a striking little horse. A beautiful charcoal except for those inky eyes. He watched Kaffy as if he was transmitting secrets to her. It was beautiful.

Water. The mare needed water. There was a faucet at the back of the stable but Kaffy supposed it hadn't been turned on in years. With her left hand she cranked at it with all her might but it was as though the tap was welded shut.

"I'll be right back," Kaffy told the mare as she took the bucket outside. She'd have to use the tap at the side of the house.

Taking these horses had been one of the stupidest things she'd ever done. Why was she so unstable? It was almost as bird-brained as the time she left a dead squirrel on the doorstep of the model home, back before she was booted from the Eternity Café. But this was impulsivity of a different color. Back then she'd been protesting a cause and she'd had nothing to lose. Now, she'd just confounded her life at exactly the time when it didn't need any further complications.

The faucet turned easily and cold water splashed and sloshed into the bucket. Kaffy could just take the horses back to the forest and let them loose, pretend she never saw them. Or maybe it would be better to call Gwen, the rancher. She could say she found them, which was true. She didn't need to tell Gwen she brought the horses home hours ago, or that she contemplated keeping the foal. What had she imagined she was going to do with the mare?

The large white horse eyed Kaffy warily as she entered the stall to hang the bucket on the wall. Did Kaffy even like horses anymore? It wasn't as though owning a horse had been a lifelong dream or anything. That fantasy had vanished as Kaffy became engulfed in the humiliations and stress of high school.

The mare dropped a few rolls of manure on the floor. Kaffy would need to find a shovel and get rid of those. Where would she hide them?

The garden. Sylvia's garden. She'd just started scratching at it just the other day. Kaffy would throw the manure on there. Fertilizer.

She heard a car in the driveway and peeked out through the stable door. It was the guests, back from their excursion. Kaffy hadn't cleaned their rooms yet. Sylvia did that chore. Kaffy needed to get inside the inn and get their bedroom cleared up before they went upstairs. She rushed from the stable as the couple disappeared into the inn.

Everything that afternoon was chaotic. After making the guests' bed and cleaning the upstairs bathroom Kaffy rushed down to the kitchen to start dinner. Guests received breakfast and dinner daily with their room charge—they were on their own for lunch. Kaffy and Sylvia usually prepared the dinner in the afternoon, washing, cutting and prepping any ingredients they needed ahead of time, which made cooking the actual meal a cinch. They'd serve dinner, then Sylvia would go home to Red, and Kaffy would take care of the evening cleaning up by herself.

Chopping an onion, her finger wrapped in yet another tissue, Kaffy prayed that Sylvia would show up tomorrow. She dried her hands on a dishtowel and tried calling Sylvia's cell phone again but the voicemail was still picking up immediately. Definitely dead.

Tonight, the guests were talkative and babbled on about their adventure in the woods hiking up to the observation station. They wanted to know if there were bears in the area, they thought they'd seen tracks. Kaffy lit a fire in the living room. The guests sat on either side of it scrolling through images of bear scat on their smartphones.

Kaffy fell into bed exhausted but it felt like hours of wrestling with her blankets and punching up her pillows before she got comfortable. Just before falling asleep she thought she heard the mare whinnying.

Chapter 5

Red opened a kitchen cupboard and peered inside. An array of canned foods stared back. Beans, soup, tomatoes. Nothing easy. He opened the fridge. An egg carton, a package of cheese, some half-finished jars—jams, salsa, pickles. Nothing he could eat. In defeat he shook frozen fish sticks onto a pan and slid it into the oven, then turned on the oven.

It was a heckuva way to end a long work day and Red's joints ached. He'd worked hard all afternoon on Kaffy's porch, plus hauled the rest of the firewood inside, and would have to go pick up another load—the inn was going to run out if the cool temperatures prevailed.

Red opened the oven door. It felt cold. Nothing happening. The door slammed shut and Red turned the temperature knob up a notch, poking the oven light on so he could sit at the kitchen table and watch his dinner cook from there.

Where was Sylvia? Had he become so accustomed to her looking after him that he couldn't fry his own dinner anymore? By the way, he hadn't asked her to look after him—she liked doing it. It wasn't always this way. He was a grown man. He'd lived in this house alone for years after Mom died. They all grew up here, Maxine, Kaffy, and Red. Their father took off when they were tiny kids, ended up in jail or something, and they mostly took care of themselves for the rest of their lives. Mom had been too young to have children. She never got over partying. She took a lot of drugs and most days just lay on the couch in the living room, smoking cigarettes and watching TV with the curtains drawn. Sometimes she had a boyfriend—those were not good old days.

The element in the bottom of the oven glowed an angry orange and Red leaned forward to get a better look but the fries weren't sizzling yet. They just lay on the cookie sheet like squared-off utility candles.

Maxine had moved to the city the minute she finished high school. She rented a place downtown with a friend and started going to the bars. She still called home regularly back then to torture Red about all the action he was missing but Red didn't think it sounded too appealing. Too many people. Too many disco lights. A bar, that's where Maxine met her husband, Glen who was as boring as a man could be from what Red could tell. But Glen fumbled into real estate at the right time and before long Maxine and Glen were a power-couple living the high life. Cocaine parties on rooftop patios—Maxine was sure to tell Red all about it. She'd never looked back, and she also never sent the family any money. Mom would've spent it on drugs anyway.

As teenagers Red and Kaffy were on their own and barely hanging on. Red remembered the fridge being bare a lot of the time and he remembered being hungry on the way to school. Gran and Pops probably helped Mom out financially but Red never knew how his mother paid the bills.

Small bubbles began to form along the bottom of the fries. The orange element dimmed and glowed at intervals. It wouldn't be long now. Red filled his vape and smoked while he waited. No Sylvia around to swat away the vapor hanging in the air.

During high school Red found a job with the local mechanic, helping out around the shop. He'd learned how to change oil, winter tires, and car batteries. After that, Red hadn't bothered to finish high school, but Kaffy did. Red could never figure out why she stuck it out because she never did anything with her education—she'd only got a job in a restaurant on the highway. Then Mom died and Kaffy moved away to the city. They never discussed what she would do with herself or how she was going to live. Kaffy had gone off the deep end in high school, and Red was so afraid of her he stopped talking to her—he avoided her. Now, he wondered if his grandparents had worried about her, a girl not yet twenty, living by herself in Toronto. As far as Red knew, they'd never tried to find her. He bet they didn't even have a phone number for Kaffy all that time she lived in the city. He knew he didn't.

A shrill blare from the smoke detector scared the heck out of Red and he sprang to his feet, grabbing the dish towel from the counter and flapping it at the smoke detector until the shrieking stopped. Then he snapped off the oven. The detector started up again the moment he opened the oven door. Dang it, dang it, dang it, why didn't Sylvia ever clean this oven? Red flailed away at the smoke detector again until it dummied up then grabbed the phone and ordered a pizza. Dang right he'd pick it up.

Dickey-Bird hopped around on the bottom of its cage, scattering seeds and making a racket. Red glanced over. "Shut up, stupid bird." The budgie cocked his head and regarded Red from one round black eye.

Red pushed the empty pizza box aside with a socked foot and stood up. Dickey-Bird hopped onto his perch and chirped in anticipation. "Okay, stupid, I'm coming."

Red examined the boxes on the shelf near the cage. Bird food. He eyed the plastic dish attached to the inside the cage. No way was he sticking his hand into the cage to detach it. Red jabbed open the side of the birdseed box with his thumb and proceeded to pour the contents of it into the cage from above. Seeds poured out faster than he'd expected and Dickey-Bird freaked out below, skittering from one side of the cage to the other trying to avoid the deluge of seeds raining down on his head.

"That oughta keep you busy," Red laughed. Good thing Sylvia wasn't around.

Red returned to his place on the couch and flicked through the channels. His eyes were burning out of his head but he dreaded going to bed alone.

Was Sylvia gone forever?

He was sorry about the fight they'd had the previous night but he was just so testy these days. He couldn't help lashing out, he was under a lot of stress. As soon as he paid off Maxine, he'd be able to relax again. Turn back into Mr. Nice Guy. Sylvia didn't deserve his moods—he knew that. She'd never done anything wrong. Nor, he gathered, had she done anything as stupid as he had.

It was all Maxine's fault. First, she'd got Glen involved, helping Red buy a laptop. Red hadn't seriously believed he could operate a computer until he casually mentioned it one day over the phone to Maxine and the next thing he knew, Glen was calling him up, bulldozing rams and gigabytes down Red's throat. "It's easy, man. If you can fix cars, you can run a computer."

Red flicked through the channels. There wasn't one darned thing on. Almost of its own accord his thumb shut down the television and he sat for a moment as the blue light in the room vanished and an uncomfortable silence surrounded him. Dickey-Bird hopped around on the bottom of the cage pecking at the drift of seeds. Hauling himself from the couch, Red picked up the vinyl cage cover and dropped it over the cage. "Don't you dare wake me up early," he ordered the bird.

Red glanced at himself in the bathroom mirror. He hadn't bothered to shave in the morning and he wasn't going to do it now, either. Without Sylvia there, what did it matter? He took up his toothbrush and scrubbed for a minute, thinking about how he ended up in this mess.

Glen had set him up with an email address. Red couldn't believe how having an email made ordering stuff so easy. He'd gone overboard, he admitted it. A bit crazy. A kid in a candy store situation. He ordered anything that popped into his head and signed up for multiple mailing lists that then dropped emails into his account suggesting more things for him to buy. So much for learning new skills.

Then Red stumbled onto the porn. In the beginning, he'd snapped it off but the images got into his brain somehow and he found himself aroused, and with nothing holding him back, well. . . until the cameras and chat boxes started popping up, he didn't think he was harming anyone. He'd only done it a couple-three of times. Then the email arrived.

Red didn't have the money demanded by the email and he couldn't put it on a credit card—Sylvia would want to know what it was for. She went over their bank statements like a hawk.

By sheer coincidence, Maxine had called that day and from something he'd said she'd intuited that Red was in trouble. Then, she'd guessed it was money he needed. Maxine was uncannily knowing. Red hated that about her. "I'll loan you some money on one condition," she'd offered.

Red held his breath. He knew where Maxine's bargains could lead to.

"You need to tell me *exactly* what it's for."

Red's face had burned in shame as his mind scrambled through a series of lame excuses why he might need some fast cash. None of them would work on Maxine. He wasn't as smart as she was nor as quick. Nothing got past her.

When Red finished explaining to Maxine about the chat boxes and video popups, he'd insisted she never breathe a word of it to Sylvia.

"You disgust me," Maxine had said. "You really do."

Red closed his eyes and shook his head. Why had he told her? Now she would hold it against him until the end of time. But to Red's surprise and relief Maxine had continued. "I'll help you out this time, Red." He couldn't believe his ears. "Forward the email to me. I'll look after it. But you close down your email, you pervert! You can't be trusted."

Red was okay with that, cripes, he was downright ecstatic. He didn't care if he was never able to order another thing online again in his whole life. He just didn't want Sylvia to find out he was a deviant. Which he wasn't. It was just a couple of times. Shoot!

"This isn't a gift," Maxine resumed. "You've got to pay me back."

"I will," Red assured her. "I will!"

"How?"

Red didn't know how. Five thousand dollars was a lot of money. "Don't worry, I'll earn it somehow." The elation he'd felt moments earlier from the thought of Maxine taking the sordid mess from his hands dissipated like bubbles in a sink. The feelings of freedom and relief popped until all that remained was scum in the drain.

"Here's what we can do. If you want," Maxine suggested. "You can pay me back when you get your share of the inheritance."

Inheritance? What inheritance? Red had never considered he was going to inherit anything from Gran, not to mention, Gran had been very much alive. The way Red understood it, any money that Gran did have was paying for her care at the rest home.

"We'll sell the inn," Maxine had said simply.

Red scoffed. "We can't sell the inn. Kaffy lives there."

"Who cares?" Maxine had tossed off. Then less monstrously, "There's no way Kaffy can keep it going and pay all the fees that are going to mount up when Gran dies. Ever hear of capital gains, Red? Plus, she'd have to buy us out, you and me. The three of us will inherit it. Don't you want your birthright, Red? Think about your future for once. Think about Sylvia."

Red filled a glass of water, swished the toothpaste from his mouth out and spat.

His mind had sifted through his options as Maxine waited for a reply on the other end of the phone. He was terrible with money. Sylvia had told him a thousand times. Even now, wasn't she trying to drag him to a money guy to figure out their retirement?

"No? Let's drop it," Maxine had said. "You can pay me back some other way."

Several uncomfortable moments of silence had passed. "The market's hot right now," Maxine nudged. "If Gran died tomorrow, we'd make a fortune."

"Maxine!" Red knew his sister was a ruthless real estate agent but this was a shocker.

"Okay, okay, have it your way, but when are you going to pay me back, Red? I can't keep a loan like this from Glen forever."

Over the following months Maxine had called often, hounding Red about when he was going to pay her back. She asked how his 'porn addiction' was coming along. Thankfully, he'd never shared much about his life with Maxine. Because the way she'd turned what he confided into a weapon, shocked him, even though it shouldn't have. He'd always known what she was capable of. Her persistence shook him so that he didn't want to answer the phone anymore. But he couldn't have Maxine leaving messages that Sylvia would hear. His rheumatoid arthritis flared—every joint in his body swelled and burnt.

And then Gran died.

"We're selling," Maxine whispered in his ear as they stood together in the funeral home. "Red, I've waited long enough."

Red's eyes blinked rapidly as he watched a small group of elderly mourners jostling around the coffee table. Maxine's elbow poked Red's ribs. He winced and took a side step away from her. "Don't worry, your secret is safe with me." She winked.

Red's conscience flared, momentarily. He watched Sylvia speaking to an old woman in a wheelchair. If they sold the inn, he could repay Maxine and she'd stop driving him up the wall. The constant stress was awful for his rheumatism. Sylvia would never know about the porno. And sooner or later he'd get used to the idea of selling Sullivan House.

"You're going to be rich. Just think of it," Maxine said, squeezing his forearm, causing him to gasp in pain. "Okay, okay," he agreed. "No problem, we'll sell."

The bedroom was still messy from the night before. Sylvia usually straightened out the bed, tidied the room, and made it nice for Red, but she wasn't there. He stripped down to his underwear and t-shirt and was about to get into bed when he remembered he hadn't locked the front door. If Sylvia came back while he was asleep, she'd have her key. Who was he kidding? She wasn't coming back tonight.

Turning the deadbolt Red spied the nail gun leaning against the wall in its box, unopened since the day it arrived. What had he been planning to build? He couldn't even remember. A deck. That's right. An outdoor deck where he and Sylvia would sit and look at the forest and the sunset. A place to keep the barbecue instead of on the grass in the backyard. A proper deck. He'd thought Sylvia would like it.

Red went back to the bedroom and straightened the sheets before climbing into bed. He would build a deck for Sylvia.

He reached over and turned off the bedside lamp.

And on top of building a spanking new deck, he would be helpful to Kaffy. When Sylvia got back from wherever she was, she'd find out that instead of being the pain-in-the-ass he usually was, he'd been supportive to Kaffy in Sylvia's absence and she'd think he was a great guy again. He'd win her back. He needed to.

Red felt better. He had a plan. He pulled the covers over his shoulder, closed his eyes, and slept like a dog.

Chapter 6

Kaffy walked a labyrinth path, around and around. Zeke was tied to a tree in the center. She could hear him whining, but also a low moan. She needed to get to him. He'd been poisoned again—like that time in Toronto. On their morning outing he'd eaten something at the far side of the dog park. Kaffy noticed him standing in the leaves chewing on something but it didn't alarm her. Someone had merely dropped a handful of dog treats over there. This was the Beaches after all—the dog to human ratio was nearly one to one.

On the way home, Zeke had started to stagger, his legs wobbly. Kaffy got around in front of him. His head was low to the ground, his neck extended, and he didn't look up at her. Then, his body stiffened and he dropped to his side.

Panicked, Kaffy shouted at people on the sidewalk and within moments a small crowd of concerned citizens gathered. "A vet lives right there!" a woman pointed at a house a few doors down.

"Can you get him?" Kaffy cried, unwilling to leave Zeke on the sidewalk.

The woman ran to the house and smashed the brass knocker against the door plate. Kaffy stroked Zeke's fur, running her hands over his furry rib cage again and again so she could feel his heart beating. Foam began to appear around his black lips. His eyes stared dully ahead. Kaffy felt as if she were suffocating.

A woman shoved her to the side. "Give me some room," she barked. Kaffy was about to push the woman over when she saw the stethoscope around her neck. The vet put the headset to her ears and listened to Zeke's chest for a second. She must have heard what she needed to hear because she snapped off the stethoscope and spoke to Kaffy as she opened what looked like a yellow tackle box beside her, "Are you the dog's owner?"

"Yes."

"What's his name?"

"Zeke."

"Has he eaten anything this morning?"

"No." Kaffy always fed Zeke after their morning walk so he'd settle down and sleep for the rest of the day on a nice full stomach. Then she remembered about the treat in the park. "Wait! No! He did eat something—I don't know what it was. In the dog park!"

The vet was already prying the lid off a pill bottle. "I'm Dr. Woodcock," she said as she popped a tiny tablet into one of Zeke's half-closed eyes.

Almost immediately, the dog wretched. He wretched and wretched until all that was coming out of him was foamy yellow bile.

"Your dog's been poisoned." Dr. Woodcock was grim.

Kaffy heard moaning again from the center of the labyrinth. It was dark. She couldn't see a thing. Another dog licked her hand. She needed to get to Zeke and save him. He'd be frightened and in pain. But Kaffy couldn't move. She was paralyzed. She couldn't turn her head to look at the dog licking her hand. Something was whimpering.

Kaffy woke up with a start.

Zeke stood by her bed. He wagged his tail and gave her hand another lick. The room still echoed with the moan, which Kaffy realized had been coming from her own chest. Her bandaged hand lay under the pillow and her entire right arm was asleep. She tried to pull it out, to wave it around and shake some life into it. She could barely lift her head off the pillow. She'd been grinding her teeth in her sleep. Her jaw ached and her neck felt stiff.

It was early, before the sun, her injured finger throbbed, and the dog paced restlessly around her room, snuffling so noisily at the crack under the door Kaffy worried he'd wake up the guests.

Sylvia often arrived at the inn early, sometimes she even brewed the coffee before Kaffy got out of bed. Maybe she was down there in the kitchen and that's why Zeke was patrolling Kaffy's bedroom like a police dog, his nails clicking on the hardwood floor.

No one was downstairs but Zeke wanted out, badly. Kaffy shushed him while she set up the coffee maker. When she opened the kitchen door the dog flew outside running straight into the darkness and back toward the stable. Kaffy heard a loud bang, which sounded like the mare stomping against the stall.

A truck's lights swept across the yard in the early morning darkness as it pulled into the driveway. Kaffy thought for a moment it was Red but Gwen, the rancher from up the road, clearly pregnant, stepped out.

"Hey Kaffy," she said waving her arm over her head. "How are you?"

Kaffy tripped down the steps into the yard and crossed quickly so Gwen wouldn't be in the sight-line of the stable. "Hey, how are *you*?" Kaffy asked, motioning at Gwen's large stomach bulging from under her jacket.

"I'm a bit worried," Gwen said, placing her hands on either side of her belly. "I've got a pregnant mare missing."

Kaffy made her face look suitably concerned, suitably surprised. "Oh no!" she said. Her innards fluttered in nervousness.

"Yea, she must have slipped through a broken fence somewhere. Went off to have her foal. They do that sometimes. I don't suppose you've seen any signs of a stray horse, have you?"

Kaffy shook her head as though she was considering Gwen's question and racking her brain for clues. Every now and then she heard another bang from the stable.

Gwen looked at Kaffy as though reading her mind. Her mouth changed from friendly to grim. "Do you mind if I take a look around?" Kaffy's stomach leapt.

Zeke appeared at a mad dash from around the side of the house. He barked when he saw Gwen and then his ears went back as he rushed over to her, wagging his tail. He distracted Gwen as she bent awkwardly over her stomach to pat his head.

"I was just about to take Zeke for a walk," Kaffy said. "You want to come along?"

"All right." But Gwen didn't look too enthused about lugging her big belly too far.

Kaffy kept a slow pace as they walked down the lane and turned left at the end, heading toward the entrance of the forest. This was Kaffy's property, or at least, Gran's property, but some acres away it backed onto Gwen's property. They walked into the forest as the dog explored in large circles around them.

"Is he always this energetic?" Gwen asked.

"Oh yea, you know how shepherds are."

Kaffy didn't know why she'd just lied about the horses. Hadn't she determined in her fitful sleep last night that it was insane to covet a neighbor's horse? She'd been reckless and impulsive to have taken them—and to consider for a moment that she could raise the foal—crazy. Gwen's unexpected visit provided Kaffy with the perfect opportunity to come clean and say she'd *just* found the horses and kept them in the barn overnight for their own safety. But Kaffy's first reaction had been to lie. And now she was so agitated her teeth were chattering. She wanted to climb the nearest tree and wait for Gwen to leave.

"What happened there?" Gwen asked as Kaffy picked nervously at the gauze around her finger.

"Oh nothing, I cut myself," Kaffy said. Her finger was hot and throbbing. She peeled the gauze back and the swollen wound was a small purple dot but it wasn't bleeding.

"Oh, that looks bad," Gwen said, sucking in her breath in a wince. "You should get that looked at."

The finger did look angry and it was so stiff Kaffy could barely bend it. She rewrapped it. "It's okay. It was worse yesterday," she lied. "I think it's getting better."

"Is it a puncture wound?" Gwen asked like she knew a thing or two about wounds. Kaffy didn't respond, just gazed upwards into the trees as if she was looking at a fascinating bird in a tree. "Did you do it outdoors?"

"No," Kaffy lied again and shrugged. "In the kitchen. I spiked it on something."

"Well, you should get to the doctor. You might need a tetanus shot."

Tetanus. Kaffy hadn't thought of that. "It'll be fine," she said even as her mind scrambled over itself in fright. "If it gets worse, I'll go to the doctor. I promise."

They arrived at the spot where Zeke originally found the horses, where Kaffy spiked herself on the fence. The dog ran over, sniffing and investigating but Kaffy kept walking while Gwen scanned the woods right to left, sporadically calling the horse's name. "Queeny! Queeny! Where are you, girl?"

The women walked a slow half-mile into the woods on the trail. Zeke did his business here and there. "I better get back," Kaffy told Gwen. "You're welcome to keep searching."

Gwen held her enormous stomach and shook her head. "I've got too much to do," she lamented. "And

I've still got to scan the perimeter of my property. See if I can find where the fence is broken."

"That's a good idea," Kaffy said, but she was skeptical. Couldn't Gwen find anyone to help her? Wasn't there a man in the picture?

They turned around and headed back toward the inn. Zeke made a mad dash past them and was out of sight in a moment.

"Someone wants their breakfast," Gwen remarked.

Why was he so frantic? Did he know something Kaffy didn't? She needed to get back to Sullivan House in case the mare was breaking down the barn.

Kaffy stood waving as Gwen climbed into the cab of her truck and backed down the driveway. "I'll let you know if I see anything," Kaffy called after the truck, as another series of bangs resounded from the stable.

As soon as Gwen's taillights disappeared, Kaffy rushed to see what was happening. Zeke barreled into the stable ahead of her. The mare nickered and snorted, hammering the stall door with her hoof, trying to break it down.

"What's the matter, Queeny?" Kaffy tried to control her fear, aiming for a sympathetic and soothing voice but the mare gave her a wide white eye.

Kaffy grabbed up a handful of hay and Queeny tore it from her as she leaned over the stall door. The foal appeared to be safe and sound. He wasn't suffering from lack of nutrition but he was making his nursing mother ravenous.

While the mare was busy pulling at the hay with her big lips, Kaffy slipped into the stall and retrieved the water bucket. It was almost empty. Again, Kaffy tried the faucet at the back of the barn but with her sore finger she still couldn't get any torque with her right hand. She threw the rest of the hay into the stall, filled the bucket at the side of the house and returned to hang it in the stall. That ought to keep Queeny satisfied until Kaffy could drive back over to the farmer for more hay.

Kaffy washed her hands with the olive oil soap Sylvia kept by the kitchen sink. The water turned the wound purpler. Tetanus? What were the signs of tetanus? A stiff jaw, Kaffy thought she recalled that fact. She wiggled her jaw. It was tense. She was tense. She wrapped her finger with gauze and taped it securely. Hopefully, Sylvia would arrive before it was time to wash the dishes.

Chapter 7

Sitting in the waiting room of the walk-in clinic, Kaffy was anxiously aware that no one cared she was unwell, possibly suffering from tetanus. Sylvia would have cared if she'd been around but she again hadn't shown up for work. Kaffy was getting worried.

She felt as if she couldn't breathe. She hated medical offices. Her mind scrambled over why it was taking so damn long to see a doctor. Maybe she needed to calm down a hair. She recalled a bit of advice she'd once received from a counselor. Take deep breaths.

The smell of the waiting room scared that idea from her mind in an instant.

Maybe there was a logical explanation for Sylvia's absence and if Kaffy was a more level-headed person she'd be able to see it. She was probably catastrophizing. Didn't she tend to go overboard about everything?

On the end table beside the row of chairs was a stack of dogeared magazines. There was no way, given the number of germs on them, that Kaffy was about to touch one but sitting right on the top, as if to taunt her, was the winter edition of *The Lonely Tripper*.

The cover showed a ski chalet—mountains in the background, a golden retriever on the porch in front of Adirondack style rockers, red and black checkered pillows, skis and poles sticking out of a snowbank. Kaffy craned her stiff neck to take it all in without picking up the magazine.

You couldn't buy advertising like that. A favorable review in *The Lonely Tripper* would fill Sullivan House for months and possibly years to come.

A nurse appeared in the hallway and called Kaffy's name. "The doctor will see you now." She led the way to a curtained cubicle where Kaffy waited nervously for what felt like a long time. Eventually, a young man came in, his white lab coat open revealing a brown checked shirt and snug fitting khakis. There was no way he was a doctor. He looked about twenty years old.

"I'm Chad Patel," he said, expertly jerking the curtains of the examination room closed. While Kaffy sat on a hard plastic chair, Chad perched on a stool and tapped a computer screen to life. "I'll just take some info from you first," he said. He spoke with a nice soothing voice. Kaffy decided to cooperate even though there was not a chance Chad could have finished medical school.

After asking a thousand irrelevant and nosy questions about her ancestor's medical conditions and her own menstrual cycle and use of medications and tapping endlessly on the computer screen, Chad swiveled on his stool, snapped on some blue latex gloves, rolled close to her Kaffy's knees, and reached for her hand.

"Now, what happened here?"

Kaffy told him the half-truth she'd prepared. She was mending a fence in her yard and a stray wire had cut her. Chad placed a gray plastic thermometer in Kaffy's ear as she spoke and after a few moments it pinged. He tapped something into the computer.

"Oh, that's nasty!" Chad said, unfurling the greenish smudged gauze, tossing it in the garbage can beside his desk.

Kaffy's finger looked twice its usual size, the skin mostly white around the cut but beyond the cut it was purplish red. The finger hurt and Kaffy almost screamed when Chad prodded it. "It's almost certainly infected," he said. "I'm going to take a swab and send it off to rule out a more serious staph infection." He left the cubicle then came back in an instant with a small tube. He pulled a stick from inside the tube and scraped it across Kaffy's finger. She shrieked. "Sorry," Chad murmured with some concern but he held Kaffy's hand firmly and did not stop swabbing.

After torturing her thus, Chad secured the stick back in the tube and turned to look at Kaffy. She was struck by his flawless skin, no crow's feet around his eyes—it didn't look like he even shaved yet. "I'm sorry, Ms. Sullivan but I'm going to have to drain it."

This was a shocking revelation. "Ugh. No! Do you *have* to?" Chad's eyes looked kind but he handed down the sentence. "I'm afraid so. You've got a nasty puncture wound. What day did you say this happened?"

"Tuesday," Kaffy wailed. She didn't have to lie about that, she remembered what day it was. Often, the days melded together, most days, it didn't matter which one it was. But Sylvia had been missing since Tuesday and it was now Wednesday. Kaffy needed Sylvia back helping her get prepared for the reviewer but what was more, Kaffy was beginning to think something terrible might have happened to Sylvia. A bad feeling ached in her bones. She thought she might fly into tears right here in the cubicle. Maybe Chad would help her somehow.

"You should've come in right away," the fake doctor chastised her. "And do you know when you last received a tetanus vaccination?"

Kaffy shook her head no. She hated doctors. She hadn't been for a checkup in years. Nothing ever seemed to be wrong with her so why would she go stirring up trouble?

"I'll give you a shot today," Chad said. "If that's okay with you."

Kaffy declined to mention to Chad the stiffness in her jaw. Her anxiety was growing with every passing moment. She wanted out of this cubicle. Her mouth was dry and the palms of her hands were slick with sweat, especially where Chad had been holding her hand.

Chad instructed Kaffy to lie down on the examination table so he could work on her hand. She thought lying down unnecessary but she acquiesced. She always acquiesced to these know-it-all men. She tried slowing her breathing, remembering some counseling from long ago. In an hour this would all be over with. She'd be home and this would be an amusing story to tell Sylvia, at least, it would seem funny, at some point in the future.

First, Chad froze Kaffy's finger with an injection. She turned to look at the wall so she wouldn't see the needle, scrunched her face, and held her breath as he jabbed her finger again and again. Next, he swabbed something wet and medicinal smelling over her hand. It stung unbearably for a second or two. Then, for a couple of minutes nothing happened but Kaffy could hear Chad moving around the small room. She peeked over just in time to see him tearing away the cellophane wrapper from a glinting metal blade. She turned her head back to the wall and held her breath. A lone tear trickled from her eye and into her hair.

"Just try to relax," Chad murmured but Kaffy could tell he wasn't paying attention to her anymore. She may as well have been disembodied from her hand. Chad was intent on conducting surgery in an examination room. Was this guy even licensed?

When it was over, Chad wrapped Kaffy's finger in a bandage and gave her instructions on how to take care of the wound. She wasn't to get it wet and she should take some pain relievers if it hurt later on. Finally, he injected Kaffy with the tetanus vaccine and sent her on her way.

Kaffy stepped out of the clinic into the fresh air. She took in great gulps of relief. The insipid overhead music was gone. The smell of disinfectants and illness was gone. She was free. She was alive. She vowed never to hurt herself again so she'd never ever have to seek a doctor's help again.

Chapter 8

Kaffy watched as a car she didn't recognize pulled into the driveway. She wasn't expecting anyone but sometimes people dropped in to take a look at the inn before making a reservation. For a few moments, no one got out. It was an expensive car, clean and shiny. Whoever was inside was one of those people who needed to make an impression with their car.

Both front doors opened at once and Kaffy was bowled over as her sister and a girl, who must have been her niece, Megan stepped out. Kaffy hadn't seen either of them in years. Megan was no longer a child, she was a teenager, and Maxine's brown hair was no longer dark brown hair, it was dyed blonde. Maxine looked like one of the middle-aged women Kaffy had served coffee to everyday at The Eternity Cafe—hair the color of a palomino, shoulder length bob with a sweep of side bangs.

Kaffy stood outside the back door, frozen like a wild animal on the road, her frizzy graying hair and faded clothes blending her into the wall of the house. She could tell Maxine and Megan didn't notice her standing there gawking—when Kaffy waved and moved toward them she saw them startle.

Then, Maxine was all teeth and lipstick and salutations. Megan followed along behind, dragging her feet as though she'd rather have waited in the car.

"Kaffy! Hello! I hope you don't mind us dropping in like this!"

In fact, Kaffy did mind. There were too many things to do today, apparently without Sylvia's assistance again, including contending with some horses she'd kidnapped. It was bewildering that Maxine would choose today of all days to stop by for a visit. Kaffy couldn't remember the last time her sister had been to the inn.

"What's going on over here?" Always the realtor, Maxine walked around the side of the house to get a better look at the unfinished porch.

"Well, it started as a simple repair," Kaffy answered, truthfully. "Then it got complicated."

Maxine laughed. "Isn't that always the way?" Kaffy supposed Maxine was accustomed to costly home improvements and jobs that overran their budgets. It was no joke to Kaffy who didn't have any spare money. The porch had become a major expenditure but she kept telling herself it would be worth it, and Sylvia agreed. Guests always commented on the porch, and the view of the forest was an all-season attraction.

Megan pulled a phone out of the pouch of her hoody and began drumming on it with her thumbs.

"Do you want to come inside? Have a cup of tea or something?"

"Sure!" Maxine said enthusiastically, as though the two sisters were long-lost besties about to embark on a heart to heart. She followed Kaffy up the back stairs into the kitchen. Megan tagged along, her head bent over her phone as she typed.

"Oh! It's been so long since I was here!" Maxine spread her arms wide and perfumey chemicals wafted from her. "It's just like I remembered!" Maxine sounded fondly nostalgic but Kaffy couldn't recall her being particularly happy here when they were young. The eldest, Maxine had always wanted to be off somewhere else, anywhere other than with her siblings, mother, or grandparents.

Kaffy poured tea at the kitchen table. Megan didn't want any—she mumbled, "I have a bottle of water in the car." She was still intent on her phone.

Maxine turned to Kaffy, "So, what's new with you?"

New? They hadn't seen each other in years. Where did Maxine expect her to start?

"I guess we'll put Gran's ashes in the same plot as Pop's?" Kaffy inquired. Maxine's husband, Glen, was executor of Gran's estate and Kaffy wasn't sure how, or who, would be making those kinds of decisions.

Were Maxine's eyes tearing up? She was looking at Kaffy with pity, as though Kaffy were a child. "Do you miss her a lot?" Maxine asked, the corners of her mouth turned down. She was wearing a lot of makeup, it showed in all the creases she was attempting to hide. Her lipstick was sparrow brown. It had left a smudgy imprint on her tea mug.

"Miss her?" Kaffy responded. "A little. But she had a good life."

"That's exactly right," Maxine said nodding at Kaffy as though she'd said something profoundly riveting. Her tastefully polished fingertips picked at the placemat in front of her on the table. "So, do you have any plans?"

"Plans?"

"You know. Now that this…" Maxine waved her hands around at the kitchen.

"This…what?" Kaffy asked.

"Well, Red. You know," Maxine said, averting her eyes.

"Red what?"

"Oh, I don't know. I don't want to get in the middle."

Now, Kaffy was dismayed. What was Maxine talking about? "The middle of what?"

"I thought Red mentioned something about taking his inheritance and moving elsewhere. That's what I *thought* I heard. Maybe not, don't quote me."

Kaffy stammered, not knowing how to respond. She didn't want to talk about the inheritance, knowing what she did about Gran's last wishes, but she also hadn't known Red had plans to relocate. He'd never mentioned it to her. Nor had Sylvia. "I don't know about that." Kaffy wanted off the subject. "I'll ask Sylvia when she shows up." Kaffy wasn't leaving the inn. It enraged her to think about it. She'd put in so much work. Leaving was not in the plan.

"So, you still see Sylvia?" Maxine asked, looking faintly surprised.

"Of course, I see her. Every day! Sylvia works here. In fact, I think I hear her car now." Kaffy hopped up to look out the window but she must have been imagining things because there was no one in the driveway. "No, I guess not." Agitated, she sat back down at the table.

Megan scrolled through pictures on her phone.

"I actually don't know where Sylvia could be and I'm getting a bit worried," Kaffy confessed. "Red told me they had a fight the other night and he hasn't seen her since."

Maxine's eyes got big. "Really? I hope nothing's *happened* to her."

Maxine's concern alarmed Kaffy. "Like what?" Kaffy asked. "What do you mean?"

"I don't know," Maxine glanced at her daughter, as though Megan's presence prevented her from saying something out loud. "But you know, Red." She made a face and her shoulders moved up and down in a skinny shrug.

Kaffy stared into her sister's mascara laden eyes. "I sometimes think I don't know Red at all," she said, trying to telepathize what Maxine was hinting at.

"Have you talked to Sylvia's friends? Her family?"

Kaffy was embarrassed to admit that she knew next to nothing about her sister-in-law. Kaffy wasn't one to pry. She didn't ask people a lot of nosy-parker questions. People would tell her stuff, if they wanted to, whether she wanted them to or not. "I would've asked them but I don't know any of Sylvia's friends. She keeps mostly to herself—you know. She's just out taking pictures most of the time."

Maxine pulled a cell phone from her oversized purse. "Her family can't be too hard to find. Their last name is Raphael, right? How many of them can there be? They're from Oshawa or somewhere like that. Maybe I can find their number." Maxine began punching letters into the screen with furrowed, sculpted eyebrows. "Hmm. Nothing coming up for Raphael in Oshawa. Do you know her dad's first name?"

Kaffy had no idea.

Megan spoke, her voice startling Kaffy who had been managing to pretend there wasn't another human being sitting at the same table completely ignoring everyone else. Well, not ignoring everything—she'd obviously been listening the entire time. Megan asked, "Is Sylvia on Facebook? Or Instagram?"

"Good idea, Hon!" Maxine looked at Kaffy, nodding.

"I don't know." Kaffy shrugged. How would she know? She avoided all that social media stuff.

"So, her name is Sylvia Raphael?" Megan's eyes flashed with teenage impatience.

"Sullivan!" Maxine and Kaffy said at the same time. "Sylvia Sullivan!" Megan raised her eyebrows at them as though they were from some previous century, which they were. She said, "Not everyone has their husband's last name, you know?" Then, "Here she is." Megan turned her phone toward Kaffy. A small round picture of Sylvia's face shone back at her.

Megan looked back at her phone and began scrolling. "Okay," she said. "The last time she posted was. . . Monday at 5 o'clock." She turned her phone back toward Kaffy. It showed a photograph of an old house and barn, Sylvia's usual type of photo. The house's windows were boarded over and the shrubs and grass were tall and unkempt. Sylvia was obsessed with the abandoned houses around the area. Megan looked back at her phone and swiped at it. "She hasn't posted anything since then," she reported.

Monday was the day before Sylvia didn't show up for work. Red said they'd squabbled on Monday night. The photo was posted after Sylvia left work. Had she taken it on her way home from work? Did she post it and then go home and get in a fight with Red? And then disappear? Where on earth had she gone?

Chapter 9

Kaffy's jaw ached and so did her finger. She popped one of the painkillers the doctor had prescribed and unraveled the copious amount of bandaging from around the wound. Her finger was less purple than it had been and the swelling was almost gone. It was probably healing. Kaffy stretched her jaw forward and then side to side as she rewrapped her finger. Her jaw was stiff but maybe she was just stressed. Maybe? She was definitely stressed.

It appeared from what Maxine had intimated that to get his share of the inheritance, which, like a pig, he assumed he was entitled to, Red planned to force the sale of the inn, and turf Kaffy out in the cold. Damn him. He'd been ruining things for Kaffy her entire life, and despite that, she'd never retaliated—in fact she'd done him and Sylvia a lot of favors. She didn't have to employ Red. She could use any number of handymen in the area. She had contacts, or she could have found someone, if she'd needed to.

Kaffy could hear Red on the porch working, but there was still no sign of Sylvia. He'd arrived just after Maxine's shiny car disappeared down the road. Before leaving, Megan had searched Sylvia's name on a number of websites but apparently Sylvia had only the one Instagram account.

If Sylvia had driven off, angry at Red, Kaffy would not have blamed her. Maybe Sylvia had come to her senses. But Kaffy thought Sylvia would've called by now to say she wasn't coming to work—Kaffy thought they were friends. And she had to wonder why Sylvia's phone was going immediately to voicemail. Perhaps Sylvia didn't want to hear from Red and had turned off her phone? Maybe she was really, really mad.

Kaffy went outside to check on how much work Red was getting done. She needed the porch finished in time for the review. Red was pulling planks of wood from the back of his truck.

"Is that for the floor?" Kaffy asked. If this was so, it was a promising development. "How long do you think it'll take?" Kaffy knew it was risky to pester Red this way and she winced as soon as the words left her mouth. Red couldn't handle pressure—the least little thing caused him to walk off the job for the day.

"It'll take what it takes," Red said, not looking at Kaffy. He hadn't shaved and Kaffy noticed how gray his beard had become. Her brother was getting old, which meant she was too. It was weird because she didn't feel old in her mind. She felt vulnerable and skittish all the time now, like a child.

Kaffy didn't want to ask about Sylvia again with Red still communicative and working steadily—she didn't want to piss him off. "No, I haven't heard from Sylvia," he said without any prompting. He glanced at Kaffy and she thought she detected a smack of remorse.

"Hmm. Well. I'm sure she'll be back," Kaffy said, although that was the last thing she was sure of. She didn't want to think about what she'd have to do if Sylvia never came back. She just wanted to concentrate on the two weeks ahead of her. But Maxine's warning about Red's threat to sell Sullivan House rattled around in her thoughts, even if it wasn't going to happen. Here he was working away on the porch as though nothing was amiss. Maybe he thought he'd fix the place up so it would sell for more money. But Maxine said Red thought the inn would be torn down, that someone would build a big new monster home on the property. Red would be apoplectic when he discovered that Gran had left the inn solely to Kaffy.

But what if she hadn't? A doubt flew into Kaffy's mind.

Gran wasn't the most reliable person. Hadn't she told Kaffy that the reason Red got married was because Sylvia was "knocked up", which turned out to be entirely untrue. What if hinting to Kaffy that she would inherit the inn was another of her not-funny practical jokes, like spelling a child's name wrong on a birthday cake, which she'd been known to do. What if the estate really did have to be split between the three siblings? If Red forced the sale, Kaffy wondered how long it would take. She had an inkling that probate, and all that sort of estate settling, took some time. A couple of years, she gathered. Practically everyone these days was going through some immense hassle with their parents' or grandparents' estate—selling family cottages, dividing assets among siblings, paying for care for their sick elders.

Would it make any sense for her to remain here while Gran's estate was in question? Why should she put in any work if it was just going to be sold? Not to mention money. It was Kaffy's money from her settlement that was paying for this porch. On the other hand, if she could prove to her siblings that the inn was a viable, stable business maybe they'd let her stay on, running it, the way she and Maxine had let Red take over Mom's house. Kaffy could pay rent to them.

She didn't have a lot of money left, certainly not enough to set up another business, or buy another house. Maxine didn't need money from the estate. And where the hell was Red going to go anyway? He'd lived in the same house down the road his entire life. He'd never gone elsewhere as far as Kaffy knew. He seemed perfectly content to live his boring meaningless life in the shadow of the forest. Anyway, Gran had left the inn to Kaffy. There was no reason to doubt it.

"You should pick a color," Red said.

For a moment Kaffy didn't know what he was talking about. Oh yes, the porch.

"Right. I was thinking brown," she said.

Her plan was a white screen door, white trim and railing, with the floorboards a practical coffee bean brown. But would that show the dust blown in off the road? She wished Sylvia was around to help with the decision.

Red's face was expressionless, as though he didn't care what color she chose. After several beats of silence, he said, "Well, get down to the building supply and pick it. I'm gonna paint as soon as the boards are down."

Kaffy was surprised. Red wasn't known to work quickly or on any kind of schedule. Was he trying to pull something over on her? Or maybe with Sylvia away, he was just trying to keep himself busy.

...

Driving toward town to pick up the paint, Kaffy passed by Red and Sylvia's house. She noted no cars in the driveway. No Sylvia. She drove on and then on impulse pulled her car over. This stretch of the road was fairly deserted. Kaffy got out, walked back toward the house, up the driveway, and whisked around the back where no one would see her.

Mom's rickety clothesline tree stood in the yard from a million years ago when Kaffy, Red, and Maxine were children. Mom had washed their clothes in a portable Hoover that bumped and gulped like a tiny brown jalopy cruising around the kitchen. After the wash cycle, which activated when the lid of the spinner went down, Mom sloshed the clothes out with a wooden spoon, stuffed them into the spin cylinder, and poured buckets of water in to rinse them. The lid closed again, the machine gushed dirty water into the drain, and sometimes all over the floor depending on if a child was "helping" to hold the snakey hose down over the edge of the sink. After the hose finished belching and dribbling water, Mom pulled the tangled clothes out of the spinner and heaved them into a laundry basket. She hung the laundry outside on the clothesline—underpants, jeans, towels—everything became stiff and a dingy shade of gray.

Red and Sylvia now owned a swanky stainless-steel washer and dryer combination unit now. Red had ordered it as a surprise for Sylvia. They must have been up to their eyeballs in debt, but then again so were a lot of people.

Kaffy mounted the back stairs to the rickety kitchen porch. The house gave her the willies. Bad memories kept her away most of the time. She peered in through one of the panes in the door's window. She could see that Red had been living like a pig since Sylvia was gone—it was only a couple of days but already dishes and trash crowded the counter. A chair next to the table sat askew, Kaffy noticed it straight away. One of Sylvia's pet peeves was chairs not tucked under tables—it drove her nuts—she always fixed them. "It just gives a room a nice finished look," she'd say.

Kaffy tried the door handle. Locked. Her breath fogged up the pane of glass. It was plain from the mess on the counter that Sylvia was not home so why did Kaffy feel so compelled to get inside? She wasn't sure, but the compulsion overruled any commonsense she might have.

When they were kids, and locked out of the house for one reason or another, they always got in through the window beside the kitchen door. Kaffy's finger hurt as she rattled the screen but it came away from the window frame easily. Would the window still lift as smoothly as it had in the old days? It did, but Kaffy knocked a plant to the floor when she hoisted the sash, and then it stuck providing her with only a narrow space to squeeze through. She climbed inside, just like when she was a teenager and Mom had locked the front door having lost track of who was in and who was still out at night.

Kaffy rescued the fallen plant and brushed away the dirt. She pounded the window closed behind her. She would not be climbing back out that way.

Even though no one was home, Kaffy tiptoed into the living room. The house was stuffy and still held the smell of her childhood, cigarette smoke and fried food. The curtains in the front window were drawn—just how it used to be when Mom lived here. A couple of empty beer cans lay on the coffee table in front of the couch. Red.

Kaffy headed toward the bedrooms then noticed on the table beside an armchair what appeared to be Sylvia's cell phone. It was! In its unmistakable case—a golden radiant sun whose center was the camera lens. Kaffy turned the phone over, the screen was black. She pressed the power button. The phone was dead. Sylvia had gone somewhere without her phone. Or was she still in the house? The hair on the back of Kaffy's neck prickled.

The house was as silent as a tomb as Kaffy walked toward the bedrooms, dreading what she would find. Could this be happening? She pushed on the door of the bedroom where she knew Red and Sylvia slept. The other bedroom doors were ajar. It creaked open. Red and Sylvia's queen size bed was an untidy tangle of baby blue sheets and a white blanket. No Sylvia.

Kaffy turned toward the bathroom. The light was on but the bathroom appeared to be empty. Kaffy whisked the shower curtain back with a screechy jangle of rings on the rod only to be relieved by the tub's emptiness. Opening the cabinet over the sink, the first thing that caught Kaffy's eye was Sylvia's birth control pills, the package she was currently taking, the pills for Monday and Tuesday still intact in the blister pack. In the drawer beside the sink was Sylvia's makeup and a hairbrush. Two battery operated toothbrushes stood side by side on the counter under the mirror. Sylvia hadn't taken any of this stuff with her when she left. Had she been in too much of a hurry? Or had she not left at all? Kaffy's heart squeezed itself like wet laundry. She hated where her thoughts were taking her. Her frightened eyes watered.

A sound in the living room sent a scurry of fear rushing down Kaffy's spine. She sucked in her breath and held it, listening as intently as possible. Carefully, quietly, she stepped back toward the living room half expecting Red to be standing there with a hatchet ready to kill her as he'd obviously killed Sylvia.

The living room was empty.

Then, a scratching noise in the corner drew Kaffy's attention. The birdcage, with the cover still on. With a great exhalation of breath, Kaffy rushed over and lifted the cover, her hands trembling. Sylvia's budgie jumped from the perch to the floor then back to the perch, taking turns to look at her out of his shiny black eyes. "Hello Richard," Kaffy said.

"...but I call him Dickey-Bird," Sylvia had told her with a giggle the day after she'd brought the bird home from the pet store.

Dickey-Bird whistled and ran his beak along the cage bars. The plastic feeder was empty. Dickie Bird cocked his head at Kaffy and jumped to the tiny swing hanging in the center of the cage.

The box of seed on the shelf nearby was practically empty. Kaffy reached into the cage and retrieved the wee dish that hung on a rail inside the cage. She filled it with the remainder of seeds. Dickey-Bird was happy and began pecking immediately, sending them flying in a happy flurry. Red would've just let Sylvia's bird die. Kaffy lifted off the water bottle, went to the kitchen, and filled it. Red was ruthless. And what on earth had happened to Sylvia? Either she'd left in a hurry after their fight, or something bad had happened to her.

The basement. Kaffy needed to check the basement. She glanced out the front window to see if anyone had pulled into the driveway while she'd been busy with the bird.

The light-switch for the basement was at the top of the stairs. Kaffy flicked it but no light came on. The bulb was burnt out. Of course it was. To let in as much light as possible, Kaffy propped open the door at the top of the stairs with a kitchen chair so it wouldn't mysteriously slam shut. She'd learned that trick as a child. The hard way. At the bottom of the stairs she knew there was another light for the basement.

Kaffy crept down the stairs, sliding her shoulder against the wall to steady herself as she went. Her knees wobbled. "Sylvia?" she called. Dickie Bird whistled loudly behind her—Kaffy nearly tripped on the stairs. "Oh, shut up, you damn bird!" she hissed.

At the bottom Kaffy felt like she might cry, she was so afraid. She flicked the light-switch on and watched as the LED bulbs gradually illuminated the basement. In the far end was the swanky new washer and dryer. Behind them, the furnace, to her right, some plastic storage bins marked "Xmas". And a bookshelf full of National Geographic magazines. No Sylvia. No dead body. No signs of a struggle. No crime scene.

My gawd, how paranoid could Kaffy be? Imagining her own brother had killed his wife. Get a grip. On the other hand, where was Sylvia? Did Red know and he just wasn't telling Kaffy? Shouldn't he be alarmed? But if he knew where Sylvia was staying, why wouldn't he just tell Kaffy? Had he done something terrible to her and hidden the body?

"Don't worry, Richard," Kaffy consoled the budgie on her way out. "I'll be back once I figure out what's happened to Sylvia." The bird nodded and swiped his beak against the perch. Kaffy glanced at the mess of seeds on the floor—budgies were messy birds. Then she replaced the vinyl cover on the cage before leaving the house by the backdoor.

Chapter 10

Through the window above the kitchen sink Kaffy watched chickens pecking in the yard while she washed the dishes. At present she possessed a stellar brood of layers and it was warm enough that Red had allowed them out to wander around, pecking at bugs and worms in the grass. It made the eggs tastier. Guests found the free-range hens a charming feature of the inn and often remarked on the flavor of the fresh eggs.

Every Saturday night Kaffy served a roast chicken—sometimes two if there were a lot of guests. She didn't know how Red kept track of which hen's time had come to be sacrificed for their Saturday meal but he must have had a system. Sylvia or Kaffy, whichever had the time, collected the eggs from the hen house each morning, and Red put a card above the nest they were to leave alone, so about once a month or so there was a brood of chicks. That way, they continuously replenished the stock.

Zeke kept an eye on the chickens as they pecked. He lay in the driveway watching, in fact, everyone watched the chickens—they were entertaining. If a predator came around, the dog chased it off, and Kaffy wasn't worried about him encountering a fox or coyote. Zeke was a brave and noisy dog when he needed to be.

Red had just finished unloading a fresh supply of firewood and had thrown an ugly orange plastic tarp over it presumably in case it rained again. Kaffy made a mental note to tell him she didn't like the unsightly tarp. The wood wouldn't get too wet once stacked. Honestly, the man had no aesthetics whatsoever.

Red stood watching the chickens and scratching at his backside through his baggy jeans. The chickens paid him no attention. Then, in a swift movement Red stepped forward and grabbed a young rooster by its head. The rest of the chickens scattered. Red plucked up the bird and swung it around in a circle. Kaffy's uninjured hand was immersed in scorching dishwater at that moment and she yelped but she couldn't pull her hand out and she couldn't look away. The brutality with which Red killed the chicken paralyzed her. The dead rooster hung limply from his hand—he was still holding it by its head.

Zeke's ears pricked forward and he licked his nose nervously, as though he'd never witnessed such a thing. Kaffy had never seen Red kill a chicken before either. Previously he'd done his dirty work out of sight. Did he know Kaffy was watching through the kitchen window?

At that exact moment Red looked straight at Kaffy. He held the chicken up like a trophy. Her instinct was to duck down but she was sure he'd already seen her. He turned and disappeared into the garage where he executed the plucking and whatever else needed to happen to make a chicken ready for roasting.

But it was only Wednesday—Kaffy wouldn't need a chicken until Saturday. She grabbed a tea towel and started frantically drying pots and wiping off the counter. Her chest hurt and she tried to not think about the poor chicken.

After a short while, Red emerged from the garage with a sack. He didn't look over at Kaffy but she stood back from the sink anyway, watching him warily through the kitchen window. There was something, roughly the size of a dead chicken, at the bottom of Red's bag. He swung it into the cab of his truck and backed down the driveway.

Kaffy wondered again about Sylvia. Where the hell was she? She shivered. It had been almost two full days now since she'd seen her. Shouldn't someone call the police? Kaffy's bandaged finger throbbed. She needed another pill. Her brain felt fuzzy. She wiggled her jaw, which was tight and achy. She felt her heart begin to beat, quicker and quicker like the wings of a trapped bird.

Chapter 11

Kaffy returned to Sullivan House with more hay. Red's truck was in the driveway but he was nowhere to be seen. More than likely he was working on the porch on the far side of the house. Kaffy pulled her car as far as she dared up onto the grass. She got out and looked around. No Red.

The farmer had been a jerk, questioning her about her need for more hay. "Another donkey?" he'd asked sarcastically. What did he care what Kaffy needed the hay for? Plus, the old geezer increased the price of a bale to $25 overnight. She hauled the hay from the trunk and headed toward the stable. As she reached for the handle, the door swung open and there was Red, his face in the shadow of his baseball cap. Kaffy froze, the string from the bale of hay cutting into the fingers of her left hand. Red spoke. "There's something the matter with that foal."

He didn't demand an explanation. He didn't even seem surprised by what he'd discovered in the stable. Kaffy's brain scrambled over itself. She wanted to rush past him, shove him aside, run headlong into the barn and see what was wrong with her foal. But she was rooted to the spot by a sudden recollection.

It was long ago, but she remembered. Red had lured her in here with the promise of a Popsicle.

Red, the man, his chin unshaven, his eyelids red rimmed, his eyes darting, licked his dry lips and held open the shed door, "C'mon. Come see."

Kaffy resisted, paralyzed with dread. All she could see was the freckled-faced twelve-year-old Red with his snickering sneer, and his nose, which he picked nightly—flicking boogers at her while they watched TV.

She was nine years old. She wanted a Popsicle.

Young Red pushed the door of the shed open and Kaffy stepped past him, never wondering how he was keeping Popsicles frozen in the heat. The barn went dark. She remembered the sound of the latch as the door shut behind her.

At least three boys fell on Kaffy at once—a thunder of smelly adolescent boys, rubbing her and slobbering on her, tugging at her shirt and shorts. Their fingers and sweaty hands, pinching and groping. They laughed in hot breaths and snorts.

Kaffy dissolved into the floorboards, sinking, spinning, birds flying in her head, a fierce flapping—and then they were off. She felt her body rising inches above the floor, as if she were floating. The boys flew out the door, whooping and laughing. Kaffy fell back to the floor, her bare bum prickling against the rough wood.

Red, the man, stared at her. "What's the matter?" he demanded. "And why're you messing around with those horses? That foal's gonna die."

Until this shattering moment Kaffy had never remembered the foul tangle of arms and legs. Forgotten? How could she have forgotten such an event? How had it been erased from her brain? Buried. *Sexual assault.* That's what it was. Those heinous horrid animals had sexually assaulted a nine-year-old, who didn't have the words for it back then, but she did now. A pit of fury burst into flame in her stomach.

"Get out of my way!" Kaffy bellowed. Red looked startled, almost petrified. She was out of control—unstable. She wanted to pick up a sledge hammer and slam him in the side of the head. Red ducked under his stupid cap and stepped swiftly past her out of the stable.

Crazed with the nightmarish memory and panicking about the horses, Kaffy ran to the stall, the bale of hay dangling painfully from her fingers. The mare was nuzzling the foal. He lay on his side on the floor. Queeny looked at Kaffy, her eyes pleading.

"It's okay," Kaffy said, her voice trembling, though nothing felt okay. "Look, I brought you some hay." She threw a feeble handful over the door of the stall but the mare ignored it, still focused on the baby.

Shit. Kaffy didn't know what to do. She vibrated with adrenaline.

Why, why, why had she brought these horses home? Why hadn't she just set the mare free? The horse would have found her way back through the woods to her ranch, wouldn't she?

Who were those evil boys?

Kaffy shuddered, remembering, at school the following day, and for weeks to come, she'd learned to make herself invisible. At recess, she'd hid in the red brick entrance way of the school, waiting for a teacher to unlock the door so she could rush back to the safety of her classroom. She didn't want to see, or be seen, by any of the disgusting boys in Red's grade.

At home Kaffy had kept to herself. No more television with the family. Instead, she'd read alone, distractedly, in the kitchen. The night after the attack was one of those rare times when Mom was between boyfriends so Kaffy had slept beside Mom's bed. Her mother probably didn't even knew she was there on the floor. The next night, Kaffy had begged to be allowed to sleep with Mom, and she must have been convincing because Mom had relented—maybe she recognized that a girl of nine shouldn't be rooming with her twelve-year-old brother. Maxine had a room to herself but it was small, not big enough for another bed. Eventually, a new man came along and Mom had him set up a cot for Kaffy in the basement.

And Red? Kaffy had avoided him at all costs. She could hardly bear to sit at the same table and eat with him. Kaffy recalled now that it was around this time that Maxine started picking on Kaffy too. She'd teased her about her hair, which had been shoulder-length and frizzy, and kind of the style back then. Maxine's had been straight and a dull brown. She'd tried to curl-iron her bangs, Farrah Fawcett style, but the curls had looked like a sausage trough framing her face. Kaffy's very existence seemed to annoy Maxine, and she complained about her all the time to Mom—Kaffy chewed too loudly, she smelled bad, she was weird and had no friends, she was an embarrassment to Maxine. Kaffy had never understood why Maxine had become so obsessed with maligning her. Everything felt wrong. Kaffy despised Red for what he'd done to her in the barn, plus he was a disgusting pig, and then she'd had Maxine and her attacks to worry about.

Mom didn't defend Kaffy. She was too engulfed in a world of pills, booze, and sleazy men. She'd wave Kaffy off with, "You're gonna have to learn to fight your own battles, Sweetie."

Kaffy had always been vaguely aware that Maxine's attention was jealousy or envy, but of what she did not know. After a childhood of ignoring her little sister, Maxine had seemed hellbent on making Kaffy miserable, and Kaffy didn't know what she'd ever done to deserve it.

The mare turned carefully in the stall so as not to step on the foal. She nosed the hay and began to munch. Kaffy slipped into the stall to retrieve the water bucket. Her heart still pounding and her mind in a trance, she carried it to the faucet at the side of the house. She glanced over at the driveway to see if Sylvia's car was there. It was becoming automatic—every time she had the chance, she checked the driveway. Was Sylvia never coming back? Where was she? What happened to her?

Red.

Red had happened to her. He'd done something terrible to Sylvia just as he'd done something terrible to Kaffy all those years ago.

And hadn't Kaffy seen the way he so callously swung the rooster around, breaking its neck? He was ruthless. Kaffy felt the blood drain from her face. Maybe she wasn't paranoid. Maybe her brother had murdered his wife. Why not? Men did it all the time, didn't they? They got drunk and enraged, threw a woman up against a wall, punched her a bit too hard, pushed and tripped her, made her fall, caused her to hit her head on something, the corner of a table, the side of a dresser. Or maybe he'd held her down, knees against her arms, maybe slapped her once or twice. Maybe she'd bit him, maybe she'd spat up at him, maybe she screamed, maybe he covered her mouth and pressed too hard, too long, covered her mouth and nose with his big rough hand and she'd suffocated. Maybe he killed her. Maybe Red killed Sylvia. Maybe it happened and the only one to know about it was Kaffy.

Maybe she needed to do something about it.

Kaffy slipped back into the stall. Her body shaking. She hoisted the full bucket of water, fumbling it back onto the hook. The foal was up on its feet nursing. Maybe it would be okay. The mare munched slowly, lowering her head to draw pieces of hay into her mouth while the foal nursed.

Kaffy patted her warm round shoulder. The mare paid no attention. She seemed calm. Maybe the foal was all right.

Maybe Red killed Sylvia.

Maybe Kaffy needed to call the police.

Chapter 12

Kaffy sat in her office staring at the screensaver on her computer, a mountain lion descending a steep trail. Her heart pounded and she felt like she was going to be sick. She didn't know if Red had done something to Sylvia, but she knew he'd done something to little Kaffy.

What if it was nothing? What if Sylvia had gone off visiting friends for a few days, just blowing off steam like Red suggested? But then why would she leave her phone behind? And her makeup? And not tell Kaffy?

Her hand trembled as she picked up the phone then set it back down on the desk, again and again. No. It wasn't possible. But look what Red had done to her, and at such an early age. Maybe he was one of those psychos you hear about who have no conscience. Maybe the chicken strangling the other day was a signal to Kaffy. He must have known she was watching.

Through the office window Kaffy saw Red's truck back down the driveway, swing to the left to turn around, and then tear off down the road. He was finished for the day. It was late afternoon and he'd been working since early morning. The guests hadn't returned yet from their day-tripping and Kaffy was alone in Sullivan House except for Zeke. In the distance she heard crows cawing, it sounded like a murder. They were making a racket, which they often did when they were attempting to scare away a predator, a fox or an owl. Sometimes, when Kaffy heard them signaling this way she followed the sound of the commotion, hoping to spy an owl sitting hunched in a tree, its head turning to and fro as the crows screeched in fury.

Kaffy picked up the phone and called the police directly. Not the emergency number. She didn't want a cascade of firetrucks, ambulances, and police cars descending on the property at supper time. She'd looked up the non-emergency number earlier. It was sitting on a scratch pad by the phone waiting for her to press in the numbers. Kaffy's stomach clenched and her head swam. For a moment when the operator said, "Police. How can I direct your call?" she couldn't remember why she was calling. She squeezed her eyes shut, held her breath and said, "I think I need to report a missing person."

"I'll connect you."

Kaffy exhaled and slumped in her office chair. For minutes a recording told her if this was an emergency to hang up and dial 911. She didn't think this was an emergency, even though her body shrieked in alarm, her hands sweating and quaking.

An officer answered and Kaffy explained as best she could that her sister-in-law, Sylvia Raphael Sullivan, had been missing since Tuesday, hadn't shown up for work, etcetera. But that was of little interest to the police officer. He wanted to know *Kaffy's* name, *Kaffy's* address, *Kaffy's* telephone number and he seemed to take a long time recording all this personal information as if he was some kind of Neanderthal just learning how to work a pencil. Finally, he asked about Sylvia.

Kaffy didn't think it was pertinent to tell the officer that she'd been by Sylvia's house and broken in through the kitchen window. When they inevitably searched the house, they'd discover all the same clues Kaffy had found: Sylvia's cell phone, her makeup, her medication.

The officer seemed disinterested, just making "mm-hm" noises every couple of seconds, and apparently not taking any notes for this part of the call—he was more interested in who Kaffy was. After a few minutes he said, "We'll send a squad car."

"Don't you want to know her address?" Kaffy urged. She didn't want a police car coming to Sullivan House. The inn didn't need that kind of attention. She thought they would just send someone around to Red's house. The line was dead. The officer had hung up.

Kaffy's stomach clenched again. Panic rumbled through her. Why had she called the police? Now she was involved up to her eyeballs. She paced around the office. What to do? What to do? The police would be snooping around here any minute.

That's when Kaffy realized the horses in the barn were about to be discovered. The police would most likely search the property. They were coming to the inn, not Sylvia's house. They'd start by nosing around all the out buildings. Maybe they'd bring search and rescue dogs.

Kaffy ran outside. The guests had not returned from wherever they were but she knew they'd be back any minute. They liked to have a couple of glasses of wine before dinner.

Zeke accompanied Kaffy as she ran to the shed. The mare seemed surprised to see them. Kaffy opened the stall and grabbed the horse by her halter. "Come on, girl. We're getting out of here."

Queeny balked, refusing to leave the stall. She whinnied, scaring Kaffy half to death. "Now come on!" Kaffy tugged fiercely on the halter. The colt was on his feet. The mare looked around at him and Kaffy lost her grasp on the halter. The mare was so strong. Kaffy scrounged around at the back of the shed for a rope to attach to Queeny's halter. Sure enough, she found an ancient leather lunge line with a rusty clip. She rushed back to Queeny and with some difficulty, because of her bandaged finger, she managed to clip the tether to the side ring of the halter. "Come on now," she ordered again in what must have been a convincing spirit because Queeny took one big step out of the stall.

"That's right, come on, this way." Breathlessly, Kaffy led the horse from the stall, but Queeny balked again at the shed door. She needed to take a good long gaze outside. She needed to look around at the foal, who was right beside her, his ears perked up like a radio antenna. Kaffy coaxed them from the barn and onto the lawn and driveway. It was then that she picked up the pace, her heart panicking as she scurried along, the mare following behind. Kaffy needed to get this horse off her property before the police arrived. She didn't know how she would

explain the fresh horse dung in the stall but she didn't have time to worry about that now.

Chapter 13

Kaffy began to jog and the mare broke into a trot. The foal frolicked along at his mother's side, delighted to be outdoors again. They ran down the path into the forest—Zeke leading the way as if they were merely taking an unscheduled but frenzied afternoon walk. When they got to the spot where Zeke originally found the horse Kaffy led Queeny around the rusty metal fence, which was tangled against the fallen tree. The horse began to graze on the shoots of grass growing among the trilliums and dogtooth violets. While she nosed around, Kaffy unclipped the lead and backed away.

The mare turned and looked at her, munching.

"Go on now," Kaffy made a wing-like whooshing motion with her arms. "Go home!" Startled, Queeny bolted, then turned and looked back at Kaffy as if she was crazy. The foal sprinted to his mother's side. Zeke looked at Kaffy, his tail lowered, confused—did she want him to go home without her?

Kaffy flapped her arms again and Queeny turned and began plodding off through the woods, the baby following along behind her.

Kaffy expelled a deep breath. She looked down at the lunge line in her hands and threw it as far as she could into the bush.

Kaffy hurried back to Sullivan House, Zeke following along behind. She wanted to get there before the police arrived. She didn't want to be seen rushing down the lane sweating and out of breath. Her throat dried up and her pulse raced as she and Zeke came around the bend. She couldn't see all the way down the driveway but she glimpsed the sun bouncing off a vehicle through the cedars. Shit, they'd beaten her here.

But it wasn't the police. It was the guests' car. Kaffy rushed into the inn to get washed up and pour them some wine. She filled a glass for herself and took a few big gulps. Maybe the guests wouldn't notice the police if Kaffy situated them in the sun room on the south side of Sullivan House. Maybe she'd be able to just talk to the police out in the yard, alone.

...

Dinner with the guests was tense. They invited Kaffy to join them at the table, which she couldn't refuse, but she expected at any moment that a police car would come barreling down the driveway and she kept looking past them, out the window, wondering if she could hear sirens in the distance.

The guests chattered on about places they'd seen—the trail horses up the road, the strawberry farm, an osprey building a nest on the top of a TV aerial of an abandoned farmhouse. None of the local attractions were open for business yet. The season wouldn't start until after the long weekend in May. Their idle blather grated on Kaffy's nerves.

The guests lingered over their meals while Kaffy sat fidgeting, unable to speak coherently. Her mind kept replaying the attack on her nine-year-old self. The floor of the barn, the slivers and the burn on her backbone, the smell of manure and motor oil, the fumbling fingers, and grunts. How had she managed to bury the memory of it so completely? Who were those boys? Why had they done that to her? What had given them the idea to attack a little girl?

Kaffy shook her head trying to clear the memory but then she recalled that the police were on their way to investigate Red and her stomach dropped. She laid down her fork. Sweat broke out along her brow. She was going to be in so much trouble.

When they were children, when Kaffy had been outraged enough to tattle on Red, he never got in trouble, no matter how egregious his crime. But he'd made Kaffy pay for her tattling later on. He'd flick her head with his bony knuckle. Or after she ate, he'd whisper to her that he'd spat in her food. Or after she brushed her teeth, that he'd swished her toothbrush in the toilet.

"Where's Sylvia?" the guests wanted to know. They'd met Sylvia when they'd checked in on Sunday. She'd told them she would see them every day—maybe take them on a hike to see one of her favorite places, a decrepit log cabin way back in the forest. She always showed her latest photos of it.

The cabin. Kaffy had forgotten about it.

She stammered. She wasn't exactly sure when Sylvia would be back. She tried to sound unconcerned, suggesting that Sylvia had gone on an extended girls' weekend, or rather girls' week. It was weak—the guests exchanged glances. They seemed miffed.

Plates rattled in Kaffy's hands as she cleared the table. She concentrated hard on not dropping dishes all over the dining room floor as she carried them to the kitchen and stacked them next to the sink. She'd tell the police about the cabin—surely, they'd sent out a search party—and that was the first place they should look.

She didn't want to think about where else Sylvia might be, but her imagination flung images of Sylvia's body wrapped in a plastic painter's sheet dumped somewhere where no one would find it, or dismembered and stacked in a freezer. The police would search Red's freezer. Kaffy felt sick.

It was dark, long past sunset, when the lights of a cruiser swept into the driveway. Kaffy was sitting by the window, waiting—exhausted and distraught. The officers remained in the car so she went outside to meet them. Their engine was still running. An enormous full moon rose in the sky beyond the forest.

As she approached the cruiser, a flashlight blared into Kaffy's eyes, blinding her—freezing her the spot.

"Are you Kaffy Sullivan?" He sounded like the officer she'd spoken to on the phone.

"I am. Can you turn off that light?"

The light swung to Kaffy's left. Two officers emerged from the cruiser, one younger, and the other a guy Kaffy knew from around the area since she was a child. He was a couple of years older than she was—Red's age, she gathered.

The hairs on her arms prickled. Was he one of the boys who'd jumped her in the shed?

It was just as before, when Kaffy was a girl, and for months after the attack she'd gone around in terror, secretly assessing every boy of a certain age or height. Was he one of them? Was he one of the boys who'd defiled her private parts and rubbed his disgusting self on her?

"Are you Red Sullivan's sister?"

Kaffy stammered, "Yea, but it's Red's wife who's missing . . . *may* be missing. I don't know." Kaffy stuck her hands in her pockets—her swaddled finger jammed and she winced. "Sylvia didn't show up for work on Tuesday, or today," she continued, shrugging and fidgety, wanting to bolt. "It's just not like her."

Kaffy felt helpless and vulnerable, as though by reporting Sylvia's absence she'd opened something up she was never coming back from.

The older cop thrust out his lower lip and gazed at Kaffy. She wanted to wrap herself in a protective shield and disappear. The young cop had his notepad out, pen poised, but he wasn't writing anything down.

"What happened to your hand?" the older cop asked. She'd rewrapped the bandage after accidentally getting it wet washing the dinner dishes.

"Oh, I cut myself chopping carrots."

His scrutiny rattled Kaffy and she felt a shirking guilt, followed by a rush of anger. She hadn't done anything wrong! Why did she always feel so blasted guilty? Defiantly, Kaffy stared him in the eye.

"Where's Red?" the cop asked.

Kaffy glared at him. "How would I know?"

"Shouldn't he be reporting his wife missing?"

Kaffy nodded intensely, crossing her arms over her chest. "I think so!"

The older cop asked a series of unhelpful questions. Had she called Sylvia's cell phone?

Obviously, yes.

Kaffy's mind flashed to Sylvia's phone in its starburst case, face down on the table beside the chair in Red's living room. The police would find it when they searched the house, that is, if they ever got a move on and started investigating!

Had Kaffy called Sylvia's friends? Her family? "I'm telling you, I've tried to find her!" The clock was ticking. Poor Sylvia might be in danger, or dying, and all these useless tits knew how to do was waste time.

"What does Red say?" the older cop quizzed her.

"I don't know. Why don't you ask him?" Kaffy snapped.

The cop stared at Kaffy. She was pissing him off. It had been her experience that men like him didn't like women like her—she wasn't kowtowing enough, wasn't cooperative. She'd had many such confrontations when she'd protested the townhouse development in the graveyard. The cops had never taken her side. They always acted suspicious, like she'd done something wrong. And that infuriated Kaffy because she hadn't done anything wrong, then or now. She was aware that people were falsely accused all the time, and punished for things they'd never done, while others were never questioned and got away with murder.

"I think if Sylvia was missing, Red would have reported it. Wives disappear on shopping trips all the time," the older cop said with an offhand finality. "If she's still missing in the morning we'll go by Red's place and get a report from him. Right now, we've got a bad accident to deal with up on the highway."

Kaffy looked toward the highway. Sometimes the lights from the cars coming down the hill through the forest were visible. Tonight, she thought she could see the flashing blue and red of emergency vehicles. "An accident?"

"Yea. It's a big mess. A horse was running on the shoulder of the road, if you can believe it, and the driver didn't see it until the last minute. He swerved head-on into the oncoming traffic. We've got a major incident out there."

Kaffy almost choked. "A horse?"

"Unbelievable, eh? It must have got loose from the ranch. Wasn't anywhere to be seen by the time we got there. But both drivers saw it. A white horse."

Kaffy's head swam. Darkness began to crowd in on her vision, her heart trampled by galloping hooves. "Are the drivers okay? Was anyone hurt?" she croaked.

"No one killed. Don't worry. But one of the passengers was pretty banged up. It could have been carnage." The older cop looked at the young cop and posed the next question to him. "Can you imagine if they'd hit the horse? Woulda been like hitting a moose!" The young cop shook his head in agreement.

Kaffy, standing on the gravel in front of them, could not imagine anything other than Queeny and the foal and how frightened they must be. It was all her fault. She should have called Gwen right away in the beginning—told her she'd found them, arranged to have her come over and get them. Instead she'd let them loose in the forest where anything could have happened. Bears, wolves, the highway—she never dreamed they'd go out to the highway.

The young cop waved a business card under Kaffy's nose. "Call me, or Hogan here, tomorrow if you have any questions," he said. "I'm sure your friend will show up."

...

Kaffy usually ignored the moon, dismissed all that tidal vibration hooey that crunchy-granola people raved about, but tonight she was energized by the full moon and the way it reflected off the birch-bark and trilliums, lighting up the forest. Zeke indulged in his usual sniff fest as Kaffy waited under a pine tree for him to finish his evening business.

Tonight's moon was the Flower Moon—Sylvia had called it that. And now Kaffy wondered if it would light up any traces of her sister-in-law—any clues to her whereabouts, any shred of her remains, any evidence leading to where Red might have stashed Sylvia's dead body. Because Kaffy was certain her despicable brother had harmed his wife.

But maybe she was wrong.

She needed to stop thinking.

If Sylvia didn't show up in the morning, Kaffy would call the police back and they'd get to work.

She wished she were brave enough to hike up to the abandoned cabin tonight. But even with the moon as full as it was, she was too chicken to go off in the darkness alone. She'd wait until the morning.

Maybe the police were right and Sylvia had gone off shopping or something like that.

They hadn’t completely dismissed Kaffy’s concerns, but they hadn't taken her too seriously either.

Dealing with the police was maddening.

It was obvious the older cop was friendly with Red.

But if he thought his male bonding crap was going to cover up yet another woman's disappearance, he had another thing coming!

“Forgive me, Sylvia, and hang on!” Kaffy prayed into the night sky.

A whispery gray cloud moved across the full moon’s face like a grimace. Shadows on the trees shuddered like bats settling. Zeke lifted his head and sniffed at the breeze for a long time.

“Come on, dog. Let’s go!”

Chapter 14

Kaffy woke early. Her first thought was of Sylvia. Then dread washed over her as she remembered Red, a freckly teen, luring her into the shed with the promise of a popsicle. She scrunched her eyes and scolded herself for being so stupid. Why had she believed him? Why had she gone into the darkness?

She cursed her brain for remembering. She just wanted to go back to yesterday when the vicious attack had never happened. But it had happened. Deep in the caverns of her mind, it had happened. Cracking open the memory made Kaffy unstable and defenseless and she hated the feeling. Hadn't she built the shell of her life by being nasty and strong? She rubbed at her temples with clenched fists. No, she preferred how she'd felt her entire adult life, up to yesterday when she'd just hated Red in general, before she'd recalled what was rotting at the bottom of it all.

Kaffy pulled herself out of bed and dressed. She still had guests to attend to. Over coffee, they told her they'd decided to leave a day early, their gaze glancing everywhere around the dining room except into Kaffy's eyes. Normally, Kaffy would vaguely wonder how she'd offended them, and whether she would catch hell from Sylvia about it, but this morning she was too shaken to care. As soon as the guests left, she called Zeke and headed for the forest.

The trail to the cabin was tramped down—Sylvia had traveled it often. Zeke ran ahead and Kaffy called him back to take the fork on the left of the path instead of their usual right.

The air was warm and a fine fresh breeze blew through the trees. Kaffy plowed after Zeke as he led the way uphill.

The cabin had once sat in a clearing, no longer. Bushes and trees had crowded closer and closer to it as the years of disuse had gone by. Woody, tangled vines covered the porch and railings, sprouting green and twirly where new growth poked through. Sylvia's photographs had captured these details beautifully. Kaffy called Sylvia's name, startling Zeke.

The forest was silent in response.

Kaffy hoped she wasn't too late. She tripped through the thick ground cover and up onto the decaying boards of the porch. "Sylvia! Sylvia! Are you in there?"

The door to the cabin hung askew. It creaked when Kaffy pushed it open and stepped inside. Sunlight from windows on all four walls streamed in as Kaffy surveyed the room. A battered table and chairs, a charred fireplace, saplings sprouting up through broken floorboards. The floor was scuffy with footprints but they could have been from a week or a month ago. Nothing seemed touched. Nothing gave any hint or vibration of Sylvia, or any other person. Zeke sniffed around the corners, sussing out each mouse hole in the wall.

...

It was shortly after nine in the morning and Sylvia had not shown up for work again. For that matter, neither had Red. Kaffy's stomach constricted at the thought of him. Kaffy plucked up the card the young officer had given her the night before, finally recalling the older cop's name, Hogan Walsh. She called the police station.

Neither Hogan nor Officer Dumbass was in yet but Kaffy was assured that one of them would get her message.

Kaffy got into her car and drove toward Gwen's ranch. She needed to know the horses were safe, that they'd made it home. If she wasn't mistaken, a bond had grown between her and the foal, a faint bond. Maybe. She wasn't sure, but the only things that had ever loved her back were animals, never people, except perhaps Sylvia.

Chapter 15

Even before Red pushed open the door to the stable, he could tell the horses were gone—their energy missing. The stall stood empty, the floor recently raked, although the smell of manure still lingered.

Outside, Red surveyed the yard and noticed a layer of straw and hay scattered over one end of the garden. He'd tilled the bed earlier in the spring but Sylvia hadn't got around to planting anything yet. Red's heart panged.

His truck was the sole vehicle in the driveway. No sign of Kaffy, or the guests, or of Sylvia.

The weather was fine, the sky high and clear, and not too hot—ideal for finishing the floorboards on the porch. Red grabbed his portable radio from the truck.

With the oldies station tuned in, the porch work was satisfying. Each piece of lumber fit snugly into place, side by each, but Red's thoughts flitted constantly to Sylvia. He'd hurried home yesterday expecting to find a message from her, blinking on the phone. Would there be one today?

Last night had been worse than the previous two nights. The emptiness of the house, the kitchen, their bed. He'd had no one to talk to, no one to share dinner with. Not that Sylvia ate a lot anymore. Red thought about his wife's determination to stick to her crazy diet of cheese and bacon, of the willpower it took to stay away from normal food. She'd lost so much weight it almost seemed impossible. Red thought Sylvia should be home by now and they'd roast up the chicken he'd brought home from Sullivan House. He paused his work and rubbed the back of his neck. For the hundredth time reassuring himself that Sylvia was okay, she wasn't in any trouble, she wasn't "missing", she was just away, because she was angry with him, because he'd been a stupid jerk—she was with her friends, or something. He'd called her mother's house last night. She wasn't there. "It's okay. She's coming back," he told Dickey-Bird, refilling the bird's dish from a fresh box of budgie food he'd bought in town. Surely, Sylvia would come back for her dang bird.

Red resumed work, fitting the boards over the cross beams, securing them in place with his power screwdriver, back and forth across the porch he worked.

Sylvia's leaving was Maxine's fault. If he hadn't been so stressed and pissy from all the pressure, none of this would've happened. He was a featherweight. He'd never been able to spar with Maxine and win. She'd manipulated him for as long as he could remember and this time, though he'd tried to outmatch her, he'd failed to come up with another way to repay his debt to her other than selling the inn. Over the past several months he'd even picked up a few lottery tickets but he hadn't won a dime. And every time he bought another ticket, he'd start fantasizing about being rich and paying everything off and how happy Sylvia would be and then they'd announce his losing numbers on TV and he'd feel helpless again. The disappointment wasn't worth it.

Red paused to rub his elbows and the sore spot at the base of his thumb. Bending and kneeling to work on the porch aggravated his arthritis but not nearly as much as he'd imagined it would. Even so, any idea of earning money this way was out the window—he couldn't reliably do physical work. Odd jobs for Kaffy were manageable—there was no pressure from her, usually, though he recalled her criticism about the logs yesterday, and her questions about his schedule, as though she was in a rush for him to finish the porch. He got it, he got it, the long weekend was not far off—guests would be arriving and she didn't want a mess of construction around—he wasn't stupid.

Gran's death had pushed Red's decision about how to repay Maxine. And Sylvia was adamant, they were not selling their house. She also didn't buy his story about wanting to move after they'd just finished fixing up their house. They didn't have to move. After the will was read, Maxine would put the inn on the market, she'd get a good price and Kaffy would just have to take her third and find another place to live. Red and Sylvia would stay in their house, he'd build a new deck and Sylvia wouldn't have to work anymore. Hopefully they'd have money to get them through their retirement.

Red felt a twang of guilt. He wished there was a way to pay Maxine back that didn't involve betraying Kaffy.

Red closed his eyes and took a breath. He pulled the vape from his pocket and took a few inhales of nicotine. He hated to remember the first time Maxine had hoodwinked him. She'd caught him in the bathroom with a girlie magazine, and told him it was illegal for him to look at X-rated stuff. Then she'd threatened to blab to Mom. Red was twelve years old and didn't realize she was bluffing. At the time he'd been too embarrassed and afraid there was something wrong with him. "Perv," Maxine took to calling him when no one could overhear. Later, Red realized how ridiculous the whole thing had been. The magazine had belonged to one of Mom's horrible boyfriends. Mom knew what men were like.

But Maxine had made a deal with a naive Red—she'd forget all about the dirty magazine if he performed her one favor. All he needed to do was get Kaffy to come inside the shed on a hot summer day—Maxine wanted to scare her.

Red had done his part. It was simple and Kaffy fell easily for the popsicle bait. But Red was as surprised as Kaffy when a gang of boys had jumped on her and pinned her to the floor. There was a tussle, it was dark and hard to see what was happening, but the boys were laughing and jostling each other and then it was over and they were up and running for the door. Red opened the door before the pack and fled. He never spoke of it to anyone. He never confronted the boys or Maxine. He just frantically pretended none of it happened, and

Maxine had stopped calling him a pervert, until recently.

Red wrestled boards from the pile and began again to lay the floor. Maxine pissed him off. She always knew his weakness. He wished he owned the courage to just come clean about it all to Sylvia. She might understand. She might forgive him.

Who was he kidding?

And poor Kaffy had never been the same after the attack in the shed. She'd always been an odd duck but she got a lot lonelier afterward. And everything about her had irritated Red. Before the attack he'd never paid much attention to his little sister but after it, he'd tormented her. He didn't know why. Maybe it was just easy—and she was there, but also, he hated the fear he'd felt when those boys piled on his sister. He hated Kaffy for agreeing to a stupid popsicle.

In high school, Kaffy had dyed her hair black and worn only dark clothes, often raggedy and torn. Sometimes people asked him what was wrong with his sister. How the heck was he supposed to know? Kaffy was an embarrassment and he hoped it wouldn't rub off on him. On the way home from school sometimes Red would see her perched high in a tall spruce near the forest. She'd sit there for hours like some deranged bird. Finally, when she climbed out one of the upstairs windows of the inn, Gran intervened and dragged Kaffy to a psychiatrist. Gran said she was worried Kaffy would jump off the roof one day.

How much of Kaffy's strangeness was Red's fault? He didn't even like to think about it. And usually he didn't, but yesterday when she'd yelled at him in the shed it had stirred up his memory. Now, years had passed, and Kaffy was here in his face almost every day. Sylvia and Kaffy were friends. He needed to accept his sister. He needed to make peace with her. And then what? Sell the inn and leave her homeless?

The sun was overhead. Noon. Red went inside the inn to scrounge up some lunch. Usually, when he was working, Sylvia made him a sandwich. But she was gone. Where was she? Why was she punishing him this long? Red slid open the glass door of the fridge and lifted the lids on bowls and containers until he found something to eat. He missed Sylvia. If she came back, he was going to make it up to her. He would treat her like a queen, and Kaffy too. He'd somehow make it up to them both.

Red tapped the final board into place on the porch and heard a car in the driveway. He dropped his rubber mallet and hurried around the side of the house to see who'd arrived. A police car.

Red recognized one of the cops. Hogan Walsh. He was the older brother of one of the boys who'd jumped on Kaffy that day long ago. Was Red never going to get away from all that? What Kaffy must have gone through—the whispers and the gossip. It had never ended for her either. He felt terrible.

"Hey there, Red," Hogan extended his hand. "How are you?"

"Not too shabby, not too shabby," Red said.

A younger cop flipped open a notebook and stood nearby. He merely nodded at Red when Red looked his way. "What brings you out here?" Red asked. His heart started to quicken and he fidgeted with his fingers. These cops weren't here on a social call. He couldn't remember a police car ever gracing the driveway of Sullivan House. Gran would not have been pleased. What would guests say?

"We hear your wife's missing."

"What?" Red scoffed and waved his hands.

Silence.

"You mean she's not?"

"Well, I haven't seen her in a couple of days. I mean, she went off on Monday night and hasn't been back, but…" Red realized how lame he sounded.

"So just a domestic squabble, then?"

"Yea, something like that." Red was ashamed. Embarrassed for allowing strangers a glimpse into his private life.

"Where's your sister? She called us about this earlier today."

Surprised, Red said, "She's not here."

"So, you haven't been in touch with your wife. . .what's her name?. . .since Monday?"

"Sylvia. No, I've tried. I mean I called her mother last night, and. . ." he trailed off.

"What about Sylvia's cell phone, you called that?"

Red remembered the barking ringtone. "Her cell phone is at our house."

The policemen's eyebrows shot up. "It is, is it? Well, that's strange. Why didn't she take her cellphone when she left on Monday?"

"Well, she was mad," Red stammered. "And she left in a hurry."

"Mad? So more than a domestic squabble?"

"No. No. Nothing major, just…" The skin on Red's neck prickled and his face heated. He felt panicky. These cops were serious.

"So, nothing major? But she's been gone without her phone for three days?"

Any confidence Red may have had in Sylvia's well-being dissolved. She wasn't coming back. He'd been stupid to think she would. She was gone.

"Do you think something might have happened to your wife, Red? An accident or something?"

"I don't know. Maybe." Red's pulse now pounded in his ears. "I haven't heard of any accidents around here."

Hogan looked skeptical. "You didn't hear about the big one on the highway last night? The horse?"

"What? A horse? Listen, I don't know anything about an accident. I thought Sylvia went off with some girlfriends for a few days. I thought she'd be back. She may be back now! Or she's left a message on my machine. Maybe she'll be back tonight. She wouldn't leave her budgie behind." Red wanted to cry. He couldn't think straight. All he knew was now he was worried sick about Sylvia.

The cops exchanged looks and nodded at one another.

"Red, we're going to ask you to accompany us to your home so we can take a look around, and then we're taking you down to the station."

"Okay." Red's body started to quake.

"Your wife's a missing person. Until we find her, we're going to have to assume something's happened to her."

Something's happened? Like what? Red supposed Sylvia might have been abducted. You heard of things like that on the news. Or maybe her car drove off the road and into the river. His mind raced with sickening possibilities.

The police eyed him peculiarly, their attitudes stiffening. It dawned on Red that they thought he'd done something to Sylvia. "Listen, I don't know where she is or what's happened to her. I guess I should make a missing person's report. Yes, that's what I'd like to do. Report her missing."

"C'mon with us," Hogan opened the back door of the cruiser and motioned Red inside. Red knew once he got in there, he was locked in.

"I'll take my own truck," he said, panicky. His chest hurt.

The younger cop placed the heel of his hand over the holster on his hip.

Hogan motioned at the backseat of the cruiser with his head. "Get in," he said.

Chapter 16

Kaffy turned off the highway and started up the rancher's lane. She couldn't bear the idea that the mare had been injured in the car crash, or that the colt was lost and alone in the forest. She needed to find out what had happened to them.

She'd forgotten how beautiful it was on the top of the hill. It had been a long time since she worked here as a teenager. Now, Kaffy struggled to remember how her employment ended—there was a shadowy curtain over her memories. She'd worked here, mucking stalls, and rounding up horses from the fields, but she couldn't remember her departure. Had she quit? Had she been fired?

A neat series of barns sat apace from a modern stone and glass house. Much had changed since Kaffy was last here. Horses grazed in the field alongside the lane. Trees surrounded it all for as far as her eyes could see.

Kaffy spied the mare—she was unmistakable out in the field with her silvery coat. The foal frolicked nearby, kicking up his hooves. Tears sprang into Kaffy's eyes when she saw him.

She stopped her car in the driveway and got out. Every horse in the field looked toward her, ears pricked as she approached the fence.

Kaffy could tell Queeny recognized her. The mare stood as still as a stone, swishing her tail once or twice while the other horses headed toward the fence, curious to see what Kaffy might have stashed in her pockets for them. Working trail horses, they were placid and accustomed to interacting with people and getting treats. But Queeny didn't take even a single step toward Kaffy.

"Hey there." Kaffy was startled by Gwen lumbering down the driveway in her rubber boots. She joined Kaffy at the fence. "You're the second one in your family to drop by this week."

Really? Red was here? Why? Had he told Gwen about Kaffy secreting the horses in the shed?

"Yea, your sister was here. Cripes, it's been ages since I've seen Maxine. It must have been high school or something. She hasn't changed."

"My *sister*? Maxine was here?"

"Yea. She told me about your grandmother. I didn't know she'd passed away. I'm so sorry."

Kaffy brushed off Gwen's sympathy. She felt awkward when people made condolences. She preferred if they didn't mention Gran at all.

Gwen nodded at Kaffy's finger. "I see you got that taken care of," she said. "Good call." She was looking at Kaffy expectantly, as if waiting for Kaffy to explain her visit.

"I heard about the accident on the highway last night," Kaffy said. "I just thought I'd come by and find out if it was the mare you were looking for the other day. Did she make it home?"

Lying to Gwen felt uncomfortable, which was strange—Kaffy usually lied with ease. Maybe it was Gwen's obvious maternity—her bulbous stomach making her look vulnerable and wobbly. But honestly Kaffy was mortified about the horses. Something catastrophic could have happened, and she would have been the one responsible. No one would have known of course, but she'd still feel terrible. It then occurred to Kaffy that there was one person who would've known. Red.

"That's very considerate of you!" Gwen gushed. Kaffy squirmed again. Gwen was entirely too saccharine for Kaffy's liking—her cheerfulness set Kaffy's teeth on edge. Didn't she know that people take advantage of women with nicey-nice demeanors like hers?

"The two of them, mother and sweet baby foal, came wandering across the field just after dawn. They must have been on their way home when the crash happened and it scared the daylights out of them. They must've run off into the forest." Gwen pointed toward the mare. "You can see Queeny's a bit thin in the ribs. But the foal seems fine. And it looks like Queeny danced a little tango with a fence or something—she's got scrapes and scratches on her head and legs. The vet's coming over later to check her over." She called, "C'mon, Queeny!"

The horse stood stock-still in the field and although the rancher couldn't have realized it, she was staring directly at Kaffy—clearly distrustful. And Kaffy didn't blame her. Kaffy was a danger to herself, and others.

"That's funny," Gwen said. "The old girl won't come over to the fence. I guess she's still spooked from the accident."

Kaffy didn't want to go inside Gwen's house for a cup of tea. She was anxious to receive a return call from the police. Also, she didn't want to try to find things to talk about with Gwen. She'd never been adept at socializing with neighbors, but she knew it was the polite thing to do. Besides, she'd almost killed Gwen's horses.

Kaffy followed Gwen into the house. It was beautiful but untidy, decorated in polished wood with soaring stone walls and floor to ceiling windows. It smelled like horses and there wasn't a sign anywhere that a man lived here. "Maxine said you guys are selling," Gwen commented as they settled onto a low sectional, a pot of tea on the coffee table in front of them. "I'm sorry to hear that."

"Selling? Oh, we're not selling!" Kaffy said. "I mean, I don't . . . Maxine said that?"

Gwen frowned, her eyebrows reaching toward each other. "I'm pretty sure she was talking about the development? She was hinting around that I should sell too. You didn't know about that?"

Kaffy stared at Gwen. Icy cold blood rushed through her body. She wanted to take flight. She wanted to set the cup of neighborly tea on the table and fly out through the nearest window.

"I was wondering what was happening with all the boarded-up places around here," Gwen remarked.

It was true—there were dozens of abandoned farms in the area around the forest. Wasn't Sylvia always snapping her melancholy pictures of them? As Gwen spoke, Sylvia's photographs swam in Kaffy's mind. Decrepit houses surrounded by overgrown shrubs, their sad windows staring, their balconies sagging. Barns with wooden doors falling off, fences askew. Driveways obscured by years of weeds spreading down the middle of tire tracks. Apple trees growing wild, blossoming their pink hearts out in May, and then dropping ripe spotted fruits to rot on the ground below in the fall. Of course, Kaffy had noticed the abandoned farms, but she'd thought the people who owned them had given up on farming and moved away. The farms weren't for sale, were they? She hadn't seen any realtor signs.

Gwen pshawed at her. "I bet the *developer* ..." Here, Gwen made air quotes with her fingers. "... is Maxine herself. She and her hubby have probably been scooping up properties around here for ages. I thought you were in on it. There's been talk of a development for years."

Kaffy couldn't summon a word to say in response. She was shocked she hadn't known what her own sister was up to but she didn't want Gwen to think she was the last to know about what was obviously a hot topic around town. What was Maxine up to? Something deceitful obviously—which she wasn't talking about to Kaffy. Was she planning to force the sale of the inn to a housing developer? And screwing Kaffy over in the process? Was Maxine the developer? Kaffy sat still, staring at her tea, trying to breathe quietly, trying to quell the speculations swirling and circling inside her head.

Gwen's phone interrupted with a loud ring. She plucked it up, looked at the screen, made a face at it, and placed it face down on the coffee table. "It's just Joan," she said. "You know her, Joan Withers? She works down at the motor vehicle place." Kaffy shrugged. "You've got your license sticker from her a thousand times." Kaffy didn't know the names of people who worked in places around town.

Gwen began telling Kaffy all about Joan Withers's troubles. It seems there was a granddaughter being bullied in high school and Joan was engaged in a battle with the school admin over it. No one took the granddaughter's distress seriously, and the boys doing the bullying were getting away with murder—writing horrid stuff about the poor girl online, sending photos of her around on their phones, that type of thing. Apparently, the granddaughter was having a hard time coping. She was going all Goth and behaving in bizarre ways. Like cutting her arms and legs—acting out, Gwen called it.

Gwen's chattering gossip astounded Kaffy and she was glad now that she hadn't yet mentioned Sylvia's disappearance. Gwen would've spread the news all over the township by the end of the morning. And that wouldn't have been right. Not when the police hadn't even opened their investigation. And besides, maybe Sylvia was coming back. Kaffy still held a sliver of hope that her dreadful gut feeling was tricking her.

As Gwen babbled on and on, the story of Joan Withers's granddaughter, so close to Kaffy's own terrible high school experience, needled its way into her brain. She didn't want to think about. It had been a grim time and Kaffy herself possessed only sketchy and scattered memories. She wondered if Gwen remembered her from back then. If she did, it wasn't stopping her from talking. Gwen's presence blurred as Kaffy's resistance to painful memories disintegrated.

It had made no difference whether Kaffy was awake or asleep—the bird dream had been no dream. Dark, as though tunnel-visioned, and noises reverberating—even a turned page sounded like fabric tearing, like a tent zipper opening. It was painful being a bird, not carefree as you might imagine a chickadee or a robin would feel, but agonizing like she was haunted—inhabited by a craven predator, alone, angry, and hurt beyond words. As a crow, Kaffy had inspected everything, considering whether to eat it, steal it, or pluck out its dead eyes.

The girls in gym class gave way as Kaffy soared past them on the track—chest and head forward, her arms trailing behind while they pumped theirs and remained upright in bright blue gym outfits. Only when Kaffy was running and breathless did the pain let up. As she ran, she planned and prioritized the materials she still needed to gather. How would she get them up inside the tree? Get the nest built before the cold weather blew in? Her classmates fled to the teacher on the sidelines, pointing and shrieking until Miss Anderson blew her whistle, and angrily motioned Kaffy off the track.

"Birds don't cry they fly," Kaffy repeated over and over as she fled from her siblings, her mother, her teachers, and the flock of idiotic teenagers that surrounded her daily at school.

Then, one day, Kaffy had woken up and the world on that morning had stabilized. A doctor had prescribed pills for Kaffy—murmured they were a type of vitamin for her brain—and they must have worked because on that day, Kaffy had awakened and the air was clear. Gone was her desire to run across the backyard toward the pine trees with her arms outspread, believing she could launch and land, balance on a branch, raising one clawed foot and then the other as she tucked her black wings against her sides.

A psychotic episode, Kaffy overheard Gran explain to her mother when she could understand human language again. She hadn't known what psychotic meant, she'd only known she was a girl again who could walk around on two legs and eat with a knife and a fork at the table.

After that, she'd kept her head down, stayed away from the girls giggling by the lockers, and finished high school.

Sitting on Gwen's couch, a full-grown woman, Kaffy reminded herself she was no longer a freaked-out teenager who believed she could fly. But her face tingled with shame.

The attack in the shed flashed through her mind. The tumult of despicable boys. *Her brother* and a gang of despicable boys. They'd violated her, harmed her forever, and stolen something from her she would never, ever recover. Kaffy's eyes watered as she tried to smother her thoughts.

Red had tormented her afterwards, every chance he'd got. He was reprehensible. She despised him.

The cup of tea cooled in Kaffy's hands but the blood racing through her body was hot and frantic. She tried slowing her breathing, telling herself, it's over, it's over, simmer down, simmer down. Hadn't she forgotten about the whole thing before? She could erase it from her mind again. She'd already survived Red once. She wasn't going to let him snatch away her stability again.

Kaffy leaned forward and set the teacup down. Soon, Gwen would stop talking and Kaffy would be able to go home. She plucked a white jelly bean from the dish on the rancher's coffee table and sunk her teeth in it. The flavor of licorice flooded her mouth and she inhaled deeply.

Chapter 17

Driving towards home, Kaffy's mind spun.

The police hadn't called back. Had they visited the inn? Or maybe they'd gone straight to Red's house to arrest him.

She took the long way. She needed to clear the confusion from her head and get her thoughts in order. She opened the car window and let the wind blow her frizzy gray hair. Clouds skittered across the sky. The sun was high and brilliant.

What the hell was Maxine up to? Was she trying to buy Gwen's ranch and build some kind of development? What about the inn? Was the Sullivan House property, which included some of the forest, part of Maxine's plan? She hadn't breathed a word about it to Kaffy, quite the opposite in fact. Maxine had displayed complete disinterest and lack of concern for Sullivan House. Kaffy's mind swirled backwards and forwards. Had Maxine and Red been plotting behind her back? Why? What had she ever done to them? Maxine had said it was Red who wanted to sell the inn and move but now it looked like she and Glen had even bigger plans. A development? What were they planning? Did Red know about it? All, this plotting and scheming was hurtful.

In one mortifying moment Kaffy realized that Glen had probably known the contents of the will all along. Gran hadn't left the inn to Kaffy. How stupid could she have been? She had no clue how estate law worked but it was likely that Glen, as executor, would know how Gran's property was going to be divided.

Kaffy felt like she was flying into a million pieces.

Like her ousting from The Eternity Café. The proposed housing development had been all over the news. When a company intends to dig up and relocate hundreds of human graves so it can build a subdivision, it gets attention. It occurred to Kaffy now that was when Maxine had started coming around. Clear out of the blue. After not seeing each other in years, Maxine had showed up at the café almost every day, chatting and sympathizing, wanting to be supportive. Had she been involved in that development too?

And then, Kaffy was lost—out on some back concession she didn't recognize, the road broken and bumpy. She needed to find her way back to the highway. She passed farm after deserted farm. Did these all belong to Maxine?

There must be a sideroad coming up soon.

Before her conversation with the rancher, Kaffy had believed these farms were abandoned because it was too hard for small farmers to make a living. When she was a girl, there were cows in these fields, and sometimes sheep. Now, the acreage where crops had grown and livestock grazed was full of weeds and wildflowers. Fences broken down, their painted posts peeling and gray.

Gwen was the only agriculturalist near the forest who was making a living from her property. At least Kaffy assumed she was making a living. There didn't seem to be a husband in the picture.

The lonely farm houses called out to Kaffy as she passed and she yearned for something intangible, something unfamiliar, something emotional, which now felt suddenly crucial. Was that how Sylvia felt? Was that why she felt compelled to preserve these places in images?

Traveling past the broken-down farms, Kaffy imagined the families that once lived in the houses. The furniture, and the beds where children once slept. Some place, somewhere, were those inhabitants now remembering joyful meals taken around tables in those kitchens? Calling their siblings and reminiscing about old times? Telling stories to their mates of childhoods spent climbing trees and milking cows?

A dilapidated white house surrounded by ancient willows looked like it was weeping. It was a stately house with tall windows, now boarded over. As Kaffy slowed to drink in the melancholy a car parked in the driveway snagged her eye.

Sylvia's car.

It took Kaffy a moment to process that Sylvia's car was parked at the end of the long driveway. She slammed on the brakes and reversed. Sure enough, it was Sylvia's car—Kaffy even recognized the license plate number.

Her heart banging in her chest, Kaffy shifted into drive and pulled up behind Sylvia's car. Fumbling with her door, she leapt out, swatting the door closed behind her. She froze. A bird trilled nearby but Sylvia's car was as silent as a tomb. Kaffy moved cautiously toward the driver's side door, terrified of what she would find.

But Sylvia's car was empty. Kaffy tried the door. Unlocked. She stuck her head inside. Sylvia's familiar scent hit her but the car was resoundingly empty.

Kaffy scanned the fields around. Nothing, nobody, just birds signaling to each other and some turkey vultures hunched high in a dead tree.

Kaffy started up the driveway, her heart thumping, fearful that at any moment she might stumble across Sylvia's body. Her eyes watered. A part of her mind pleaded the case that Red had killed Sylvia, while another part argued, if he did, why was Sylvia's car parked in this laneway, with no signs of a struggle?

The house was silent but the porch let out a loud crack when Kaffy stepped onto it.

She called Sylvia's name.

The door to the house was boarded over but Kaffy was able to peer through a window pane. Inside were cobwebs and gnawed damage from mice and other creatures. Otherwise, the house looked untouched. And empty.

But on the floor, over by a window—were those scuff-marks in the dust? Kaffy moved along the porch toward the window. Some of the boards had been pried off and leaned neatly against the house. Just as Sylvia would have arranged them. Was she in there?

Again, Kaffy called Sylvia's name.

She twisted her body so she could reach up under the boards covering the top half of the window to the lower sash. She pushed on it and the window lifted easily. Just like the window had at Sylvia and Red's house, the window she'd crept through when she was a misbehaving teenager, and also, the same window she'd crawled through the other day when she broke into their home in search of Sylvia. But this window wasn't sticky enough in the side jamb to lodge itself, and there was nothing nearby to hold it up. Kaffy contorted herself to push with one hand while she stuck the other hand underneath. For a moment she endured the full weight of the window while maneuvering her other hand down and wedging it beneath the window. Her large wrapped bandage helped, even though every time her finger bumped, she winced.

At last, Kaffy got the window open wide enough to climb through but she needed something to keep it propped open. The boards leaning against the wall were too long to work and not wide enough. Her shoe. Kaffy let the window down and pulled her shoe off. Then she went through the entire procedure again but this time when she got the window open a ways—she stuck her shoe in at the side, toe to heel. It worked to hold the window open. Good thing she'd worn her heavy hiking shoes today and not her floppy runners.

Fortunately, Kaffy was skinny enough that her lower half squeezed through the window without too much trouble. Her hands landed on the dusty floor. It was dim inside the farmhouse but not dark. When she got to her feet, Kaffy could see that someone had boarded over the windows on the front of the house, on the porch, and in the door, but light shone in from other sources. There were footprints in the dust on the floor. Kaffy moved cautiously along them.

"Don't come in here!" a voice croaked weakly from the far room. It was Sylvia, hoarse but unmistakable.

"Sylvia, it's me!" Kaffy cried, rushing toward her sister-in-law's voice.

"No! Don't come in here!"

Kaffy swung around the doorway but stopped in her tracks. Sylvia was set in the middle of the kitchen, only her torso visible. From the hips down she disappeared into broken floor boards. Her SLR camera lay on an unbroken segment of the floor in front of her. "The floor is collapsing," she cried when she saw Kaffy.

A kitchen table, on an angle, pinned Sylvia in place. It must have fallen through the floor at the same moment she did. Sylvia was pale with dark circles around her eyes, her lips were whitish and chapped. "Do you have any water?" she pleaded.

Oh God, she was dying of thirst.

Kaffy had no water. But she . . . "Sylvia, I've been looking for you everywhere! How long have you been here?"

Sylvia shook her head. "I don't know. Feels like forever. Water, Kaffy, water. Where's Red?"

The breath caught in Kaffy's chest but she pressed her lips tightly together, a burst of fury flaring inside. Red, the monster, hadn't spent one iota of his time worrying about Sylvia's whereabouts. He'd been willing to accept his own stupid theory that she'd left him after their fight to visit her friends—without her phone and without her makeup! Red was a demon. How was it possible that Sylvia still cared about a man like him? He was callous and cruel. He hadn't technically killed Sylvia, but his neglect and lack of concern would have if Kaffy hadn't been driving by trying to unscramble her crazy thoughts of despair and self-pity.

"I'm going to get you out of here," Kaffy told Sylvia, feeling brave and determined. "You just sit tight."

Sylvia smiled weakly at Kaffy's unintended joke. "I don't have much choice."

Kaffy lay down on the floor. "I saw this on the internet one time. It's what you're supposed to do if your dog falls through the ice." Kaffy pounded on the boards ahead of her, everything seemed solid. She wormed toward Sylvia, dragging herself by her elbows. When she got about a foot away from Sylvia, the boards seemed different, punky, and sound absorbed into them when she pounded. "I think the floor here is rotten."

"I'm pinned by the table," Sylvia said, twisting her body and pushing at the wedged table in a futile gesture. She'd probably tried this maneuver a thousand times already in the past couple of days. "And I can't feel my legs." Sylvia looked at Kaffy, her eyes frightened.

Kaffy scooted and squirmed in the opposite direction until she was across the kitchen behind the table. The floor beneath her seemed solid so she got to her feet. She inched forward, one step at a time, until the table was within her reach. Then she grabbed it underneath and gave it a pull. A great crash and puff of dust filled the kitchen. Sylvia screamed and Kaffy knew she'd killed her. "My camera!" Sylvia shrieked. The table came down hard on the camera, spinning it across the floor.

Sylvia began to cry. "Oh my God, I can move," she gasped. "Don't come any closer!"

Kaffy watched anxiously as Sylvia flung her body sideways and using her elbows labored out of the hole. When her legs were free, she rolled until she was on solid floorboards. Kaffy hurried around the perimeter of the kitchen. "Just lie still there! Are you okay?"

A rank odor arose from Sylvia's jeans, which were torn and crunchy with dried blood and urine.

"Sorry." Sylvia grimaced as Kaffy inspected her legs. "I peed my pants several times." Kaffy waved off her sister-in-law's concerns and Sylvia giggled. "At least it wasn't number two."

Kaffy shook her head in admonishment but was thrilled that Sylvia's sense of humor had survived. Sylvia's legs were badly scraped on the outside of her thighs. "Can you wiggle your toes?" Kaffy asked, looking at Sylvia's shoes as though she would be able to see through their rubber tips. "Yes!" Sylvia announced, wagging her feet back and forth. Kaffy exhaled the breath she didn't know she'd been holding. Sylvia bent her knees and grimaced.

"What? Is something broken?"

"No, I'm just really really stiff. I've been cramped in that position for so long I think my muscles atrophied." Kaffy helped Sylvia into a sitting position. "Kaffy, I'm so thirsty. I need some water."

Kaffy wasn't one of those tote-a-damn-plastic-water-bottle-everywhere-you-go type of person.

"Do you have any in your car?" she asked Sylvia.

"I don't know. Maybe."

Kaffy was about to leave and run down the driveway to Sylvia's car in search of a water bottle when it occurred to her to try the taps in the sink.

She made the outer edge tour of the kitchen again to reach the sink. She turned what she guessed would be the cold water and the pipes responded with the sound of a tortured cello. A spurt and a spray and then water began trickling. What could she pour it into? Kaffy opened the cupboards but they were bare. Whoever had lived here before had taken away every trace of themselves, except for the kitchen table.

Kaffy scrubbed at her hands in the cold water to clean them. With her bandaged finger it was almost impossible.

"Hurry," Sylvia called. "The sound of running water is killing me here!"

Kaffy cupped some water in her bandage-free hand and toddled methodically around the edge of the kitchen to where Sylvia now sat. Kneeling, Kaffy held her hand in front of Sylvia's lips. She drank noisily. "More," she sputtered.

Kaffy rushed back to the sink and filled her hand again. Then back to Sylvia to drink. Back and forth she carried water until Sylvia waved and said, "Okay. Enough for now. Let's get out of here."

Chapter 18

Sylvia was too weak and her legs too badly scraped to crawl out through the window so Kaffy yanked open the front door of the house and kicked through the planks nailed across the doorway. She wasn't the strongest person in the world and kicking and wrestling the lumber took a long time. Sylvia slumped on the floor cheerleading and telling Kaffy she was a hero.

When the space was large enough, Kaffy helped Sylvia to her feet and propped her up as they staggered off the porch to begin the slow walk down the lane to their cars.

Midway, Sylvia cried, "My camera!"

She'd forgotten it in the farmhouse on the floor. She yanked on Kaffy's arm as though determined to go back and fetch the camera herself. "No," Kaffy said, leading Sylvia forcefully past her car to Kaffy's. She opened the door and guided Sylvia into the front seat. "I'll go get it."

Sylvia's head was leaning against the headrest and her eyes were closed when Kaffy returned to the car with the camera. "We'll come back for your car later," Kaffy said, reversing down the lane.

There were no vehicles in the driveway when they arrived at Sylvia and Red's place. No police cars. No Red.

Kaffy helped Sylvia inside the house to the sound of Dickey-Bird squawking. "Oh, he missed me," Sylvia crooned. "Will you feed him, Kaff? I need some water."

After drinking at the kitchen tap, Sylvia lumbered towards the washroom. "I've got to peel these jeans off my legs somehow."

Kaffy topped up the budgie's seeds then waited in the hallway outside the bathroom—asking through the closed door if Sylvia needed anything. She didn't, but she was taking forever. Kaffy leaned against the wall, drumming her fingers.

She had a lot to think about, and none of it happy. She was certain now that Gran had not left her the estate. How could she have been so naïve? Glen was the executor of the estate. He knew the contents of the will. Maxine and Red were going to force Kaffy to sell and steal away her home and livelihood, only to enrich themselves. But the question she couldn't wrap her brain around was, why? Why would they do that to her? Why would they do that to their sister when they each owned their own homes and had spouses for support? They knew Kaffy had no other place to live, no one she could depend on. Sullivan House was the only thing Kaffy had. She'd spent years caring for Gran, who was their grandmother too, and they hadn't lifted a finger. Well, Red had helped out now and then but only *after* Gran went into The Home.

Kaffy could have spent those years finding a job, or a husband with a job, although truthfully those ideas seemed far-fetched now. Or she could have invested in another business with the money from her settlement—instead she'd helped out Gran, and continued the work Gran and Pops had started when they were newly married. Why were her siblings being so greedy and ungrateful? She could almost understand it coming from Red—he was a shithead—and it wasn't like he was living in the lap of luxury in this cramped little house with Sylvia. But Maxine? She already had everything money could buy.

Kaffy, pondering her siblings' treachery, paced the short hallway between the bathroom and the bedrooms. She considered what might happen if Red walked in the door right this minute, and how much she'd like to clobber him.

Sylvia emerged from the bathroom in her housecoat and let Kaffy help her into the living room. She sat down gingerly on her chair and picked up her cell phone, which was still sitting where Kaffy left it the other day when she broke in. "Guess I should have taken this little item with me," Sylvia laughed, waving the phone. "I was in a rush to get out to the countryside while the sky was still gloomy, you know? I love it like that—the light up there by the farms—it's just spectacular." Sylvia looked up at Kaffy, color returning to her cheeks. "I hope I didn't cause you a big hassle. I know you think I'm crazy."

Kaffy's heart squeezed. Sylvia was crucial to her. Over the past few days, she'd realized just how much, and not just because of her contribution to Sullivan House. Kaffy loved her sister-in-law. She loved someone. The truth of it staggered her.

"I just hope the pictures turn out," she said. Sylvia smiled.

"You should go home, Kaffy. I'll be fine here by myself."

Kaffy wouldn't hear of it. She insisted on making some food. Sylvia hadn't eaten in days and although she claimed she was indeed hungry she wasn't starving, keto diet, you know, but Kaffy doubted that was true. Sylvia agreed to bacon and a cheese omelet but she didn't want Kaffy to go to any trouble.

As Kaffy fried bacon in the kitchen she recognized the twang of the hinges in the front door. "Sylvia?" Red's voice boomed.

Tongs in hand, Kaffy peeked her head around the doorway and saw Red stepping into the living room doorway followed by the policemen she'd met the night before. "You're back!" Red cried.

"Oh my gosh, Red you wouldn't believe what happened to me!"

Moments of awkwardness zigzagged around the room as the officers took in the scene, nodding in Kaffy's direction, acknowledging her presence. Sylvia looked questioningly from the police to Red.

Hogan handed a set of car keys to Red. He seemed aggravated by the sight of Sylvia in a terrycloth housecoat with freshly washed hair sitting safely in her armchair. "Next time you slip out, do us a favor and let your husband know where you're going."

Kaffy gasped and Sylvia looked confused and then hurt but the cops had turned and were lumbering out of the house. Red stood in the doorway, shuffling his boots as if he didn't know what to do.

Pressing her lips tightly together, Kaffy turned back to the sizzle in the kitchen and shoved the bacon around the pan. It burned her up that Red appeared unflappable. Had the police confronted him? Or had he called them, *finally*, after days of Sylvia's absence? Tongs still in hand, Kaffy poked her head back into the living room. "Your wife was *missing*. You realize that, don't you?" Red looked over at Kaffy as though noticing her for the first time. He looked back at Sylvia. "What?"

"She was injured!" Kaffy shouted. "And you didn't care!"

Kaffy couldn't hold back any longer. She'd tried to suppress her anger, to not let it rip in front of Sylvia, who seemed oblivious to the fact that her asinine husband hadn't been concerned when she didn't come home for three nights!

"I *was* worried about you," Red defended himself to Sylvia. "I called your mother last night, to say I was sorry about the fight and . . ." He trailed off. Obviously, he hadn't done enough and he knew it.

"What are you talking about? Fight?" Sylvia looked confused.

"The other night. We had words. You know. I'm sorry!"

Sylvia shook her head. "Oh, for heaven's sake, Red. I'd forgotten all about that. Anyway, thanks to Kaffy, I'm home!"

Kaffy fumed silently as Sylvia recounted the story of how she'd been out taking pictures of the old house. "I know, I know, I should've told you where I was going." Sylvia had seen what she thought was an orange and white cat running up the lane so she'd parked her car and ran after him. "I thought it was Hugo!" By the time she got to the house, the cat had disappeared and Sylvia wondered if he'd found a way inside. She pulled the boards from the window on the porch and crawled into the house. When she stepped into the kitchen, the floor collapsed, and she went right through to the basement ceiling. At the same time, the table fell on top of her and she was trapped there, dangling.

"Oh my God!" Red knelt beside Sylvia's chair and stroked her hair. In all the years Kaffy had seen them together, she'd never witnessed a tender display from Red. "Were you scared?" he asked.

"The first night was terrible," Sylvia recalled. "I was cold and scared and my legs stung like crazy. I was yelling my head off, but of course none of you could hear me. I think I must have fallen asleep. The next day was awful too. I kept thinking I was going to die."

The smoke detector over Kaffy's head screeched, freezing the blood in her veins. Bacon was curling into black ribbons on the stove. Kaffy pulled the pan from the element. "Shit, shit, shit!"

Red slunk into the kitchen. "Sorry, it's a mess around here," he said, clattering the dishes around in the sink and shoving some papers over to the side of the table.

Kaffy's heart pounded. Proximity to him rattled her. She wanted to blast him but she was terrified to start. Her thoughts raced. She might never stop. Finally she blurted out, "Am I the only one who didn't know our sister was buying up the farms around here?"

Red stared at her. "My sister?" he asked, stupidly. "Maxine? What are you talking about?" Red's confused face told Kaffy in an instant that he wasn't part of it and his ignorance cooled the flame inside her somewhat. But she repeated what Gwen had told her. "Think about it. The horse ranch and Sullivan House must be two crucial pieces of a pretty large development plan. I think Maxine is trying to get hold of it all!"

"I don't believe it," Red scoffed. Kaffy's blood boiled again. He always brushed her off like a pesky fly.

"So, you're telling me you aren't part of Maxine's plan?"

"What are you talking about, Kaffy?"

"To sell the inn!"

"What? Why? Who said that?" Red looked guilty and upset.

"*You* did! The other day. You said, now that the will is being settled, we're going to lose the inn."

Red stared at Kaffy. "You're nuts. I never said that." He looked away and swept some crumbs onto the floor. "And I swear, I'm not part of some big development plot." Red yanked the freezer door open and stared inside. Over his shoulder Kaffy could see a chicken, trussed and wrapped in a plastic bag, possibly the one he'd killed the other day. "Anyways," Red said. "Can we talk about this later? Let's get my wife some food."

Sylvia gobbled down the bowlful of tuna salad Red fixed for her and then yawned widely. Red helped her to her feet and held her as she limped toward their bedroom. Kaffy sat on the couch fidgeting with the bandage on her finger, angry and confused.

"She would've died out there if it hadn't been for you," Red said, sitting down across from her. "I can't ever thank you enough for finding her."

Kaffy's eyes filled with annoying tears and her fury betrayed her, scattering like a flock of birds over the forest. Never in her life, had Red said a kind word, and now that he had, she didn't like it one bit. She had every right to hate him til the day she died.

Before she could get to her feet and flee from the house, Red spoke. "Kaffy," he said looking down at his hands. "There's something that's been bothering me for a long, long time and I need to get it off my chest." The look in his eyes was nervous but determined.

Kaffy froze. Whatever Red wanted to confess—she didn't want to hear it. Not now. Whatever it was, how dare he bring it up? If it was the attack, he could just shut his filthy mouth right now because she wasn't ready. Her brain had only revived it yesterday. Screw him!

"Do you remember the time when you were little and I told you if you came in the barn, I'd give you a popsicle?"

The room spun. Kaffy couldn't breathe. Her ears rang. "I always wanted to tell you," he said, leaning forward. "I didn't know she was going to do that."

Kaffy wasn't hearing properly. Did he say, "She"? What was he talking about? She? A bunch of boys had jumped her—Red among them!

"She said she just wanted to scare you. I've always felt terrible. She tricked me too. I had no idea. I know it's no excuse. If I'd known those guys were hiding in there, I would never have done it." Red shook his head, as if in disbelief. "Maxine had sibling rivalry bad," he said. "Or something."

A hot tear landed on Kaffy's hand and her body shook. "I'm going now," she gasped, standing, wobbling. The floor dipped as she headed for the door.

"Are you okay? I'm sorry, Kaffy. I'm sorry . . ." The screen door slammed behind her, cutting off Red's words.

Kaffy tumbled into her car. A van blasted its horn, swerving to avoid her as she backed out onto the road. She felt blind and disembodied. The world was slipping off its axis. She needed to get home. Home? Where was home? She felt like she was never going to feel safe again.

Chapter 19

Zeke was sitting in the driveway when Kaffy pulled into Sullivan House but he moved out of the way when he saw her car. Kaffy parked and sat, staring blankly over the steering wheel for a long time as Zeke paced outside, waiting—waiting for her to return to her senses. Finally, Kaffy opened the car door and Zeke nudged his snout under her hand before she could even step out.

Kaffy took a deep breath, consoled by Zeke's loyalty. The poor dog had been home, alone, guarding the inn, worrying about her all afternoon. "Hey there, good boy. Did you think I was never coming back?" Kaffy scritched behind Zeke's ears. "I'm sorry I took so long."

Most nights, Zeke slept on the floor in the hallway outside Kaffy's door but that evening, after she'd eaten leftovers from a container, standing at the fridge with the door open, he'd followed her into her room and laid down on the small rug at the side of her bed. Kaffy leaned against the headboard staring into space. Absently, she thumbed the novel she was reading on the bedside table. It was impossible to concentrate on anything other than what Red had just said: *Maxine* had planned the attack on Kaffy. Every time she looked at Zeke on the floor, he thumped his tail, watching from his deep dark eyes, his eyebrows raised in concern. Kaffy patted the covers and invited the dog onto the bed. Normally, Zeke wouldn't be interested in sleeping so close but tonight he jumped right up. He stood unsteadily, then walked around in a circle and dropped into a tight knot, his tail tucked under his back legs. He laid his head on his paws and blinked at Kaffy.

"Good boy," Kaffy said, patting Zeke's head. It was comforting her to have him so near, so protective, as if he knew how vulnerable she was tonight. Kaffy turned out the light and lay listening to the spring evening beyond the window, an owl hooting, birds fretting before bedtime, a mysterious animal chattering, a coyote's howl.

...

Kaffy spent the next morning distracting herself from a creeping sense of despair by cleaning the inn like a madwoman for the weekend's guests who would be arriving around four o'clock. Sullivan House was quiet, an echoing muteness as Kaffy labored around the upstairs, wheeling a vacuum cleaner behind, scrubbing the bathtub and shower stall. After the housework, she gave a few minutes of thought to the evening meal, and then went out to sit for a rest on the porch. She felt hollowed out—as if her body was alive but her brain had shut down.

How could Maxine have set her up to be attacked like that?

They'd both been so young.

What would have possessed a sister to do that to another sister?

The porch furniture was still scattered on the grass beside the newly floored porch. Kaffy lugged up a chair and sank into the creaky wicker. A crow called from high in a tree. The caw-caw-cawing felt like an urgent message from a long ago time.

Up until yesterday, Kaffy had thought only that her childhood had been loathsome—her memories general and indistinct. But now she remembered with a frightening vividness that she'd hated the way she'd looked; she'd fought with the terror in her head; and she'd despaired over the family she'd lived with. After the attack, she recalled, she'd vowed never to let anyone hurt her again. She'd trusted no one, kept herself apart, and said mean things to other kids. When puberty hit, and to her vexation, Kaffy's body had sprouted a couple of alluring areas, she'd wielded it in some kind of perverted vengeance, allowing boys to take her behind the school or into parked cars where they pawed under her t-shirt and slobbered over her face and neck. All the while, she lied to herself—she didn't care! She pretended she was laughing at their pathetic groping. Pretended she was getting even by being in control.

In high school, her brain had broken—just cracked in half or something—she'd thought she was a crow for crissake! She'd taken medication, and it had taken a while to get back to normal, but after that she really had become an outcast. The boys whispered *slut, slut,* and the girls turned away at their lockers. An aloneness engulfed Kaffy.

In contrast, Maxine, a few years ahead of Kaffy, had flounced around the high school like a prom queen, having no trouble dating boys or making oodles of giggling, gossiping girlfriends.

From the porch, Kaffy watched a crow lift from atop a tall spruce and fly off deeper into the forest.

Mom had died. And Kaffy had graduated—somehow collecting enough credits. And then, not long after graduation, after screwing up another job, Kaffy had packed a bag and left for the city. She hadn't given a moment's thought to Gran and Pops, and she didn't care how Red felt about her departure. She didn't mean to stay away forever, to never visit. It just worked out that way.

Maxine had never come home either, as far as Kaffy knew. She'd married Glen Beryl wearing a dress whiter than white—with one of those feathery things on the side of her head—in a Presbyterian church Kaffy suspected they didn't attend, by a reverend they'd probably just met that day. The reception had taken place in a tacky banquet hall with dancing all night to top-40 disco, spun by a DJ with buck teeth and a too tight suit jacket. Kaffy had attended the wedding solo—sat in the church near the back, dined at a table with the other singles, including the DJ, where she got drunk on the cheap wine and fled home before the garter was flung.

Kaffy sat rocking on the inn's new porch. The boards hadn't been painted but they were neatly in place, tongue in groove—an impeccable job. Red's handiwork. Zeke lay beside Kaffy's chair as she rocked.

Did she even want to be here anymore?

The question rattled the cage door in her brain.

It felt as if her dreams for the inn had died overnight. She didn't care anymore about the reviewer, in fact she had half a mind to call up and tell him not to come, that Sullivan House was closing. She felt utterly defeated.

Kaffy picked at her wrapped finger, the bandage frizzy and gray from the morning's housework. Why had she taken those horses? Why couldn't she control herself and behave like ordinary people did?

She rocked some more.

This view, she liked. She liked the trees on the hill. Correction, she loved the trees on the hill! They were her cherished ones, her companions. Walking in the forest cathedral was the closest feeling to acceptance Kaffy possessed.

She patted Zeke's head and he thumped his tail against the floorboards. She loved this dog at her side.

Red's truck turned in the driveway. Zeke leapt off the porch to go greet him.

Kaffy froze, her stomach queasy. She wondered if she had time to run inside and hide. It hadn't occurred to her that Red would come back or that she'd have to face him again. Overnight, her world had dissolved—as if she'd fallen off a cliff—as if she'd never have to see anyone in her family again. Why was her brain making her feel like she'd died?

Sylvia emerged from the passenger side of the truck and instantly spotted Kaffy sitting on the porch. She held Red's hand as they walked toward the porch. Another stunner. Kaffy had never seen them hold hands. Maybe Sylvia's disappearance had altered something in their relationship.

"Beautiful morning!" Sylvia called, her usual sunny, optimistic self, seemingly unshaken by three days trapped and injured in an abandoned farmhouse.

The weather was glorious. Kaffy almost hadn't noticed. The sun licked the treetops on the hill, and remarkably, the shrubs and maples around the inn were covered in leaves as though they'd unfurled overnight.

"Coffee on?" Sylvia asked, mounting the steps.

"No, but I'll make some." Kaffy began to rise but Sylvia patted her on the head and breezed past her into the inn. "No worries, I'll get it."

Red stood looking at the trees on the hill, his hands in his pockets. "You okay?" he asked.

Kaffy looked away. Did he really expect her to believe he wasn't culpable for all the shit he'd done to her over the years? She inhaled sharply to cut off a wave of emotion that threatened to topple her.

Uncomfortable minutes passed until finally Kaffy rose and went inside. Sylvia intercepted her on the way from the kitchen with three mugs on a tray. "Come on," she told Kaffy, "Get the door for me." Reluctantly, Kaffy followed Sylvia back out to the porch. She didn't want to talk. She didn't want to be here anymore.

Red carried the other rockers onto the porch and Sylvia sat down between the two siblings. Each stared off into the forest, mugs of coffee in hand. Kaffy wondered how long they would sit here. She felt ready to take off. She wished she could follow that soaring bird.

Sylvia broke the silence. "Red told me some things last night." She was gazing straight ahead. Kaffy stopped rocking and held her breath. "First, he told me about Maxine buying up all the farms around here and how he's worried now that the inn is part of her plan." Sylvia paused. She frowned and glanced at Red, then at Kaffy, as if deciding whether to proceed. "And he told me about Maxine setting you up to be ambushed by a gang of boys when you were just a little kid." Sylvia's chin quivered and her voice broke.

Kaffy put her hands over her face. She didn't want to talk about it. Not with Red here.

"He told me Maxine blackmailed him into helping her. He didn't know, Kaffy, he didn't know!"

Kaffy breathed shakily, her mind refusing to accept what Sylvia was telling her. It was fine for Sylvia to believe Red, but that didn't mean Kaffy had to swallow his lies. She kept her eyes closed. She didn't know what to think. Her memory was hazy and mostly visceral. Had Red stood apart in a darkened corner of the stable while the other boys held her down? Kaffy couldn't remember. She didn't know.

"I'm so sorry that happened to you," Sylvia said, patting Kaffy's arm, startling her. Kaffy's eyes flew open. Sylvia was looking at her sorrowfully. Kaffy looked away.

No one spoke, which wasn't unusual. None of the three were talkers. For a while, they sat looking at the hill and the forest, at the birds floating between the treetops, at the clouds drifting by in the wide blue sky. Kaffy thought she might choke—her throat was so tortured.

Sylvia said, "Kaffy, listen, we want to be partners with you, whatever happens."

What was Sylvia talking about? Partners? In what? Didn't she realize Kaffy's plans for the inn were now poisoned? Maxine was going to force the sale and that was that. In Kaffy's mind it was as good as done. She was going to be alone again, and on her own. That was okay. She'd done it before. She didn't need a family. Besides, in a year's time, this countryside would be destroyed by a blanket of Maxine's ticky-tacky houses, identical boxes distinguished only by their shingle color or which side their two-car garage was on.

"I love working at Sullivan House," Sylvia continued, oblivious to the tortured thoughts in Kaffy's mind. "And like you always say, it has tons of potential!"

Kaffy shook her head. It was never going to happen now. She'd been a fool to imagine otherwise.

"Whatever happens," Sylvia said. "You've got a home with us, right Red? We'll fix up a bedroom for you. Don't worry, we're with you. We love you."

Red said nothing and Kaffy didn't dare look at him sitting there chewing at his fingernails. She'd be mortified if he even tried to confirm what Sylvia claimed. Sister and brother had never loved each other, had never uttered those words. Kaffy, in fact, hated Red. It wasn't possible that his deplorability was a figment of her imagination. She wasn't mistaken.

Words croaked from Kaffy's throat, "I don't think I'm sticking around here." As she uttered them a hatchling of resolve broke through inside her. "I'm going to head off somewhere else." Maybe she'd buy a property. Raise some bees, and chickens. She'd always wanted to tap sugar maples.

Sylvia closed her eyes and shook her head, her face dissolved in sadness. "Whatever you need to do, Kaff," she said. "Just remember. We love you."

Kaffy shook off Sylvia's improbable words but something crumpled inside. She gripped the arms of the rocker. She would not cry. She would not cry. This was not happening.

Chapter 20

Gran's lawyer worked from a Victorian house on a corner lot in Whitchurch. Kaffy followed Sylvia and Red inside and sat down on a leather lounge chair. Maxine and Glen had not yet arrived.

Sylvia sat across from Kaffy, watching her intently as if willing her to stay calm. A noisy corner of Kaffy's mind argued that the honorable thing, when Maxine stepped through the door, was to lunge for her throat and kill her.

Kaffy had agreed to drive down for the reading of the will with Sylvia and Red after an emotional week of picking through the past and exploring tenuous plans for the future. Kaffy and Sylvia had traversed the sorry years of the Sullivan family history while preparing food for guests and tending to the inn as usual. Sylvia was kind and supportive, never pushing Kaffy further than she was willing to go. Kaffy backed away from the meandering conversation many times, overwhelmed and anxious, but in the end, Sylvia assured her enough that Red had not taken part in the attack on her in the shed—he'd been the duped doorman, and a remorseful one at that. Kaffy's memory of the boys on top of her was sensory but indistinct, she couldn't rely on it, so by the end of the week she'd made a decision to trust what Sylvia told her, one day at a time, giving herself the option of changing her mind any day she liked.

Norton Johnson emerged from his office, shook hands all around, and offered solemn sympathies about Gran. He was a nice man—wavy hair, dandruff on his navy suit jacket shoulders, and with more heft than a man of his age ought to carry. Maxine and Glen were late. Norton said he'd check back in a few minutes. Did anyone want coffee?

It was painfully quiet in the waiting room—no piped-in music or radio.

"Guess who came back today?" Sylvia whispered loudly across the space. Kaffy responded by raising her eyebrows. "Hugo! My cat, he came back! He was at the kitchen door this morning, meowing!" Sylvia's elation was infectious and Kaffy was truly glad to hear about Hugo. "I guess he's forgiven you for the oysters," she laughed.

"And guess what I heard?" Sylvia continued.

Kaffy waited expectantly for another piece of bright news, which Sylvia seemed to attract like bumblebees to a flower. "Gwen had her baby! A boy. A few days early but everything's fine." This too Kaffy was relieved to hear. She'd tried phoning Gwen once or twice over the past week but the call had gone unanswered.

The waiting room lapsed back into silence. Other than these newsy bits from Sylvia, nothing could be said without the receptionist, or somebody lurking in the shadows of the office doorways, overhearing. So, they sat quietly, studying the ugly paintings of mountain scenes on the walls.

Ten minutes later, Maxine, with Glen following, burst through the door in a huge phony flurry. Her perfumed presence filled the office as she gushed apologies at the receptionist before turning to greet her siblings with a fake smile and concerned face. It was obvious to Kaffy that beneath the surface, Maxine was vibrating with exuberance—celebrating this day when she would lock up the final piece of property in her big real estate scheme.

In the past week, Red had confessed to Sylvia about some porno email, which Sylvia had tried to explain to Kaffy. The gist of it was tied up with the will, and the estate, and a loan to Maxine—whatever—Kaffy didn't care anymore. All she knew was that Maxine assumed she had Red in her pocket and she was in for a surprise because he wasn't. The other day, Red had made a promise to Kaffy. He'd vowed that whatever they decided to do, they would do together—they were a united front, and Maxine couldn't force them to do anything.

Kaffy promised nothing in return.

Glen shook hands with Red, and nodded toward Sylvia and Kaffy. Maxine was not put off by the sedate expressions and cool reception they were receiving even from Sylvia. None of it fazed her. She was the big sister. She was in charge. She began firing inane conversation-starters at the group in general. "What's everyone been up to? Anything exciting?" Kaffy pressed her lips together and stared across at Sylvia's knees.

Norton appeared and shook more hands, offered more condolences, then led the Sullivan siblings into a shabby boardroom. Gran had conserved her resources by not wasting money on a fancy attorney—Norton Johnson simply supplied Whitchurch with divorces, leases, and wills—all the mundane stuff.

Kaffy seated herself as far from Maxine as she could. She didn't even want to look across the table at her sister. Maxine took the spot next to Norton, clattering her car keys down on the hardwood, staking her position. Glen pulled out the chair on the other side of the lawyer—important guy, the executor of the estate.

After again offering coffee, tea, water, no, no, no, Norton Johnson began to read Gran's will. He read carefully and methodically, all Gran's cryptic messages, her quirks and foibles coming through in the reading. Kaffy's heart panged with loss. She missed her grandmother. Gran had been true to herself, and Kaffy needed to aspire to that.

"The domicile, known as Sullivan House, at 14736 Highway 24 in Simcoe Township, is left to my three grandchildren, Maxine, Reginald, and Katherine Sullivan," the lawyer read.

There it was. As expected. Kaffy's heart hurt.

Norton paused and glanced at each face around the table. Kaffy averted her eyes, ashamed. At least she'd never confided in anyone that Gran had promised she'd be pleasantly surprised by the will. No one would ever know that Gran had pulled one final switcheroo on her youngest grandchild. Kaffy gulped hard. Her chest felt as if it was caving in and her stomach swallowing itself. What a fool she'd been. She wanted to cry.

Before Norton read again, he got up from the table to retrieve a scroll from a desk in the corner. The room was hushed as he unfurled a large document onto the table, setting paperweights and a water glass on the four corners. Kaffy oriented herself to the yellowing rendering and recognized it as a bird's eye view of the Sullivan House property. She could see where the highway sliced through the forest and a broken line marked the border of Gwen's ranch and Gran's lot. It was all so painful. Her eyes swam with tears.

Norton picked up the will and continued reading, clearing his throat before finishing the final portion. With his pen, Norton drew attention to the forest section of the drawing. "The remainder property, demarcated as section 4, adjacent to 14736 Highway 24," again he tapped the paper. "I leave to the Government of Ontario to conserve for perpetuity and future generations as forest and parkland. It is to remain greenbelt and may not be developed."

If a spider was walking across the carpet at that moment, everyone would have heard it.

"What?" Maxine demanded.

Kaffy looked at Red in confusion. He was looking at Sylvia whose hand now covered her mouth. A grin began to spread across Red's face and he met Kaffy with dancing eyes.

The facts of the matter hatched slowly in Kaffy's mind. She stared down at the map again and then back at Red. Gran had left the inn, the building, which couldn't be worth all that much, to her three grandchildren, but the forest she'd left to the province.

"Glen!" Maxine shouted. "Did you know about this?" She was on her feet, her chair thrust behind her. She gathered her leather purse and her car keys.

"Of course not. I'm just the executor." Glen's face was white and his eyes looked frightened.

Norton Johnson interrupted. "I know you must have a lot of questions and I'm here to answer them. There are some specific instructions I'll need to go over with Glen but we have some time now if you want to ask me anything."

"I can't believe this!" Maxine sputtered. "Is it even legal? Leaving your property to the *government*?" She spat the last word like it was a curse.

"Your grandmother didn't give the property to the government," Norton corrected her patiently. "She left it to the Province. The government, no government, will be allowed to interfere. I did quite a bit of research to get that part just right for Mrs. Sullivan. She was adamant she wanted the land to be preserved for generations to come."

Kaffy's mind swirled, astonished.

Did this mean Maxine's development was dead? Without the crucial piece of land was her plan ruined?

Maxine grabbed her purse and stormed from the office. Glen watched helplessly as she fled. Red and Sylvia clasped hands on the boardroom table.

A memory fluttered into Kaffy's mind of Gran tucking her into the backseat of Pop's old Volvo. A teenaged Kaffy was wrapped in a scratchy gray blanket, frightened and sick, her heart hammering in her chest. Her eyes were streaming tears and her throat felt raw from sobbing. Minutes earlier, Kaffy had perched on the edge of the Sullivan House roof.

Somehow, Gran had reached out through a window and pulled Kaffy inside just before she could take flight. Now, Gran was bending over Kaffy, fastening her seatbelt as if she were a child. Gran's scent swirled around Kaffy and Gran's words reached into her soul. She kissed Kaffy's forehead. "You're safe, my dove. You're safe now. Gran's right here."

~ The End ~

Acknowledgements

Thanks to Nancy Day for her constant support and careful reading. Thanks also to Big Shirley and to Pat Murray who read early versions of this story. To all the women who have written in workshops with me over the past year, your encouragement sustains me.

About the Author

Sandy Day lives in Georgina, Ontario, Canada. She is the author of several books. When she attended York University, way back in the last century, her professors included the great Canadian writers Michael Ondaatje and bp nichol. Sandy is a creative writing workshop facilitator, trained in the AWA method by the Toronto Writers Collective.

Books by Sandy Day

Fred's Funeral
Chatterbox Poems
An Empty Nest
Head on Backwards, Chest Full of Sand

Visit **www.sandyday.ca**
for a free Ebook

Made in the USA
Coppell, TX
12 August 2022